A SM

MW01205280

Gentlemen of the Coast Book 1
by
Danielle Thorne

CHAPTER ONE

Savannah, Georgia
1792

THE LEAVES OF AN ANCIENT oak tree fluttered in the quiet inviting Christine Fryer to dismount inside the safety of its low, sprawling arms. She tied her chestnut horse to a limb and peeked between the swags of dripping gray moss until certain she was alone. The grassy marsh around the inlet lay quiet. *No pirates here*, she thought.

With a shrug at her silly precautions, Christine left the oak and neighboring cottonwood trees to tramp through the damp cordgrass, careful not to trip into muddy puddles leftover from the last tide. She had only a short time until Papa noticed she was missing.

Taking a deep breath, she glanced back at the safety of the grove then continued toward the low banks of Sandpiper Inlet. Birds clucked over the occasional sucking and popping sounds of life inhaling nourishment from the wet earth. Springtime perfume wafted along the musical breeze, mingling with sea salt and the pungent scent of plant rot.

Inhaling, Christine allowed the warmth of the late morning to soak through her pleated riding jacket. Her brother,

Matty, had told her he'd spied pink blossoms flowering across the marsh's flat expanse like pantaloons, and she wanted to find some to press out flat and preserve.

This nature hunt was a good distance from the cobble-stoned streets of Savannah but a perfect excuse to leave the house. Papa watched her like a hawk. He criticized the books she read, the embroidering she attempted, and even her taste in fashion. If she was not making calls or being called upon, he thought she was wasting time, and to him, time was money.

A low hum drifted through the air that was not mosquitoes or bees. Christine looked up as she reached the bank along the brackish water. She recognized the sound as blended voices and peered across the inlet to the other side. Two men stood on the distant shore near a small skiff bobbing up and down in the shallows. A tall heron tiptoed nearby.

The conversation across the marsh grew loud, making Christine squint in the April sunshine. One man looked squatty and rough in his old weathered hat and bell-sleeved tunic. He also wore a gun belt crossed over his chest. She hesitated mid-step.

The other man towered over his companion. He was broad-chested and muscled with a thick headful of dark umber hair. He frowned then jerked his thumb over his shoulder. "...waxing moon," he insisted in a loud voice that carried across the wetlands. The shorter companion shook his head and said something that must have mollified the other.

They didn't look like fishermen. Whatever could two men be doing discussing their business here?

The taller of the two, dressed too neatly to be out gathering clams or crabs, replaced a fine cocked hat and without warning glanced her direction. Christine froze. She realized she looked like an eavesdropper, but this wasn't anyone's land. The marsh around the inlet was too wet and dangerous to build upon.

The squatty man saw her, too, and his mouth dropped open. With a look of unhappy surprise, he splashed off through the water to climb into his skiff. The clamor made the heron take flight. It launched itself over the water, unfolding its enormous wings as it glided past Christine's head.

She should have turned away and pretended to be preoccupied, but instead, she glimpsed back after the bird's departure. The tall fellow had not waded out to the boat with his friend. In fact, he stood opposite her with no more than a furlong of water between them. He stared at her from beneath his hat as his mouth melted into a forbidding line. Christine realized with a start that he had familiar bright eyes—and a hand on the belt around his waist.

Noting the light sword at his side, she knew she'd interrupted a meeting intended to be kept private. Pirates? The coast and waterways south of Savannah were lately rumored to be the hunting grounds of Alligator George.

The man frowned, and she stumbled a few feet backward, her black riding boots tripping over mounds of grass as her straw hat slid awry. He looked offended and perhaps angry. Uncertain if she knew him, for he seemed like someone she should recognize, she turned on her narrow heel and hurried across the lumpy ground toward the trees. When she glanced back, she saw the mysterious gentleman had disappeared, but a tingling warning crawled up her neck, and she realized he was coming around the inlet's point.

She'd been a fool. To leave home without Abigail or one of the stable boys and wander away from town was rash. Besides roaming criminals or a threatening band of Indians, she'd put herself at risk.

Frantically jerking the knot loose on the rope, she threw it over the gelding's neck and scrambled up onto the horse in the most unladylike of positions. Branches overhead creaked, and she skipped the stirrups and kicked her feet.

"You! 'Vast, there!" someone called.

The man broke into the grove of trees and darted forward with a grim look on his face. Christine yelped and slammed her boots into Janus's side. Sensing her fear, the old horse lunged forward and carried her off wildly while she clung to the reigns and his mane. With one last hurried peek over her shoulder, she saw her pursuer had stopped.

He stood with a black boot planted on an overturned tree. The look of fury on his face turned the air in her chest to ice, and she urged Janus to go faster back down the game trail. There was no reason to stop or pretend to be friendly. She lowered her head to keep her hair from blowing across her face and dug in her heels.

CHRISTINE PICKED UP her fan but stopped to stare into the looking glass. She grimaced. Mr. Hawthorne was old, balding, and tottered back and forth when he walked. If she didn't find someone soon and settle down, Papa would marry her off to him by the end of the year. Why couldn't she catch the eye of a Talbot boy?

"Miss Christine!" Abigail rushed into the room with a look of panic on her face. "Your papa is waiting for you." She stopped short when she found Christine studying herself. "Don't you like your curls? You look beautiful. It's time now."

Christine forced herself to look agreeable. She'd hardly recovered from her near-murder in the marsh. Even retiring to bed early the night before and focusing on the ball today had not helped her forget about it. Her legs were sore from riding astride so fast and for so far. She shuffled down the stairs with Abigail behind her. She hadn't slowed the horse to change her seat until she'd seen the rooftops of town.

Abigail had nearly combed her hairless unknotting the tangles, but throughout the ordeal Christine said nothing. She'd had no business going that far out alone, not with pirates about. It was her own fault, and she feared breathing a word of it would cause a great deal of trouble. Better to wait, she convinced herself, until she knew for sure if Alligator George was lurking nearby or it was just uncouth, wild men up to no good.

With a throat that felt full of wool, she followed Abigail downstairs and outside. The luxurious coach rattled around as the servants tried to calm the horses. Mathew, or Matty, as she had always called her brother, had arrived home from his business on the river to ride with them but seemed impatient. Papa was plopped back on the tufted cushions looking irritated. Christine swallowed, took the hand of the nearest stable hand, and let herself be lifted into the carriage.

"It's about time, Miss Fryer," growled Papa. He glanced up at the early moon hanging over the grasping trees then tapped his cane on the side of the carriage. "While I don't want to be the first to arrive at Blakemore House, I certainly won't line up behind the commoners." He snorted. "They have invited nearly all of Savannah, you remember."

Commoners? thought Christine. Weren't they all common now? "I'm sorry, Papa," she said in a whisper.

He shook his head the way he did when he was disappointed with her, and the carriage gave a giant heave across the cobblestone road. They'd already quarreled over Christine's feelings about another ball. It was only April, and she was exhausted. Every time she walked into a room, the gentlemen examined her like she was a horse for sale.

And then there was Richard Hawthorne. It was no secret Mr. Fryer wanted a match with the wealthy Hawthorne family. They'd been planters before the Revolution and now were invested in some of the local merchants, too.

Matchmaking. She hated it. She'd much rather strike up a remarkable friendship or dance her way into a passionate affair—either if they led to lifelong happiness—than be arranged into a marriage with a man twice her age.

Christine frowned as she fanned herself in the stuffy carriage. The night air felt only slightly cool, and it was heavy with damp sea air. If the party was as large as Papa expected, Blakemore House would be crowded with bodies that smelled either too strongly of perfume and powder, or not strongly enough. She would suffocate in the scented heat.

"Your gown fits well," said Papa, glancing up from his conversation with Mathew. "Thank you." Christine glanced down at the cut of her bodice that felt close to immodest. Papa insisted she wear the latest fashions. She turned her attention to her brother. "You look handsome, Matty. I daresay you won't have a moment alone unless you flee to the card room." She teased him to make herself feel better. Perhaps he would stay at her side and chase away any old widowers interested in merchants' daughters.

"I promise to enjoy myself if you do." Matty gave her a meaningful look and a wink. He didn't seem any happier to be crowded into the carriage with a lecturing Papa than she. "The Lovells will be there, and I heard Miss Dolly Fenton will be as well."

"Oh, Dolly. Yes." Christine felt her shoulders relax even as Papa made a noise in his throat to remind her that Dolly was one of her acquaintances that he felt too common. "I haven't seen her since Christmas, and she did write she would be here this spring to help her aunt through her lying-in.

Papa frowned at Christine's mention of Mrs. Fenton's delicate condition, but she shrugged it off. What did he expect raising her with so many boys and without a mother? Her stepmother, Prudence, and her newborn half-brother had passed away three years ago from complications in childbirth. She felt alone as ever.

"Do not hide in the shadows tonight, Christine," came Papa's expected decree. "I did not order new gowns and trimmings for you to hide from all of our friends."

Christine gazed out the carriage as if the view of Savannah's tall narrow houses set shoulder to shoulder captivated her. By "friends," he meant Mr. Hawthorne. All of the planters, the merchants, and aristocrats were their friends because they all gave the Fryers their business. In Papa's esteem, the ones who were single, no matter their age or temperament, should be her focus. He would not waste his only daughter on just anyone when he could use her as an investment.

CAPTAIN NATHANIAL BUTLER strode down the street with boots smacking against the cobblestones at each determined step. His destination, Blakemore House, rose across the square, tall and proud over its neighbors just a stone's throw from the river. The three-story monstrosity had a tall, wide door at the top of a high porch with a set of curved iron stairs on either side. With all of the lights shining from the windows, the red brick stones seemed to glow like a distant star.

He stopped under a live oak tangled with the dripping coastal moss and tugged on his cravat. His carriage was not in the best condition, certainly not enough to roll into town and stop in front of the Blakemore's, so he'd ridden a horse to the port, tied it off at a tavern, and walked his way toward one of the wards of Savannah's elite.

Overdressed plantation owners and wealthy merchants crowded up the steps and flowed into the large home. Nathan took a deep breath and let it out in a slow stream to push his concern about the girl at the inlet to the back of his mind. He thought he knew her, but it happened so fast he could only hope that she hadn't recognized him—or that she'd mention what she witnessed. He and Isaac would have to avoid the marsh for a time in case anyone came out to investigate his business.

A shrill laugh drew his attention back to the soiree spilling out of the house. Right. Business. He only needed to greet everyone with his best smile, boast of his good fortune trading up and down the coast, and pretend to be unlucky in the card room. Perhaps losing a few games to an aristocrat or two would endear him to the older, affluent men of society. They had not been fans of his father.

Nathan squared his shoulders and joined the arriving throng rife with women. Young ladies sparkled in their pearls and gemstones. The gowns—fabrics from the East Indies sometimes acquired illegally—made them look like fairies. Aggressive, scheming ones. He suppressed an inward groan as he darted around a fine carriage and then pretended like he'd just stepped out of it. Despite the numerous ladies with hope in their eyes and lies on their lips, none of them would give Nathan Butler of derelict Clearwater Plantation more than a moment's passing glance. He snorted to himself. What did he care? Love was a waste of time and dangerous to boot.

"Captain Butler," said the hostess with a deep curtsey. And there she was—one of the reasons he carried bitter feelings toward the opposing sex.

Mrs. Pricilla Blakemore fluttered her eyelashes as he bowed and made an escape past her elderly husband, down the hall, and into the crushing drawing room. Music pitched across the high ceiling from the other room and made the flickering candles on the walls dance. He took a deep breath and accepted a drink from a servant in livery passing through.

Wasting no time, he emptied the glass and went in search of another. Along the way, he spied his friend—and secret business partner—inside the ballroom speaking with two well-dressed women. He maneuvered through bodies, ignoring the pleading gazes of the wallflowers and their chaperones' pinning stares, and joined Mathew's circle near an open window that let in a blessed breeze.

"Captain Butler," said the redhead in delight, and he grinned and took her hand to kiss it although for the life of it he could not remember her name.

"You came after all." Mathew looked pleased.

"I couldn't miss the most important ball of the season," lied Nathan. He could miss it, because it did not make him money or new contacts, but he had to show a certain face in Savannah if the Butler reputation was to improve along with his income.

Mathew threw an arm around his shoulder. "Did Captain Butler tell you, Miss Newsome, that I beat him in a horse race along the river last weekend, and he owes me the finest bottle of wine that can be found?"

The young woman raised her gloved fingers to her lips and smiled at Mathew. "Did you now, Mr. Fryer? Beat poor Captain Butler so soundly? I did not hear of it."

Nathan gave a one-shouldered shrug. "I fly better with sails." Both women would probably know that he commandeered a ship, he was still a poor dead planter's son, and a mad one to boot.

Mathew clapped Nathan on the back. "Yes, and you wouldn't know Captain Butler fought aboard a commissioned war vessel. I happen to believe he was polishing coppers and serving out gruel rather than at the guns."

Miss Newsome gave a sorrowful smile and slanted her head. "Poor, poor, Mr. Butler." She enunciated the word "poor," and Nathan bristled. She could only assume the Butler family was still poor. Young ladies did not loiter around the docks or do business in the warehouses. Many people had no idea how well-to-do he was since the Revolution. He'd become a capitalist in its ashes—no planting rice fields for him. Only those lately invited to Clearwater Plantation would know of its restoration.

Mathew wiggled a brow at him in mischief, understanding that not all of the marriage-hungry women in Savannah realized the Butler family was doing exceedingly well.

Nathan smiled as the musicians raised their bows for the opening dance. "And I dance poorly, too. It's the minuet, my fine friend," he said to Mathew with pretended pleasure. "I do know how you love to dance." He dipped his chin and bowed, glanced at the two women anxious for Mathew's arm, and darted off before he was obligated to ask one of them to take the floor. Let Mathew be forced to choose.

Smirking, Nathan exited the ballroom while patting the cards in his pocket. He'd come to play really. A few games lost to establish trust and others to win to show the old guard he was not some young pup. Reaching the polished narrow staircase, he looked up and found Mrs. Blakemore on the landing surveying her glittering kingdom. She gave him a knowing stare that bloomed into a sultry smile, and he spun around on his heel to find the back courtyard and fight the crowd there instead.

IT TOOK THREE DANCES in a growing swelter before Christine could escape from the ballroom and creep up the stairs. She stood on the top of the Blakemore's second floor and glanced over her shoulder at a room that had to be a study of some sort. Smiling at a gentleman who made it up the stairs with a little wobble in his step, she backed away from peering over the banister for Dolly and stiffened her back.

It was stale in the house, and she was perspiring beneath her shift. Scrunching her nose, she tiptoed down the long hallway, staring at paintings on the walls to look thoughtful. The unwelcome stair-climber waddled straight across the landing into her room—the one she'd been intent on exploring. Murmuring voices came from behind the door as he shut it. She crumpled her mouth into a frown and tiptoed down the hall to a window that overlooked the garden between the Blakemore's and their next door neighbor. There was also a slanted view of the street. It looked like everyone in Savannah was cramming into the house.

Seeing no sign of Dolly, Christine ignored the people arriving outside the window and crept toward the last door in the hall. She turned the lavish brass knob. When it creaked, she froze, but hearing no one, slipped inside and shut the door with a quiet click.

"Christine?"

She looked around in surprise. Matty and another gentleman were sitting across from one another in front of a low fire. The only window in the room hung halfway open and chatter from outside drifted in and stirred around the silence.

"Matty?" He looked distressed. Upset. She narrowed her eyes at the man across from him as vague recognition budded in her mind. It was his old friend, the man from outside of town. He sat with his legs crossed, a head taller than her brother, broader and darker, except for a set of startling blue eyes. They glowed in the reflection of the firelight. Those eyes. She'd admired them before. His cravat was untidy, and he looked too comfortable with himself.

Mathew jumped to his feet and cleared his throat. "Nathan, I mean, Captain Butler, you remember my younger sister, Miss Christine Fryer?" Mathew scowled at her. "She's supposed to be dancing."

Captain Butler looked bemused. He stood up with a loud exhale and gave her a little bow.

"Captain," she stuttered. "It's been some time."

He raised a brow like she'd insulted him, and his rugged, devil-may-care handsomeness thunked her in the back of the neck like a heavy stone. Christine swallowed. Regardless of her recognition of the Butler man, she was unsure why he was hiding in a room with her brother. Papa would certainly find *him* common.

Both of the gentlemen stared at her. Taking the hint, she let herself out with a curtsy and a meaningful scowl directed at Mathew because he wasn't downstairs either. It wasn't fair.

She stepped into the hall and returned to the window. It had a deep ledge that made a perfect seat to watch the carriages rattle by. Across the street, shadows slunk into the ward's park, a lovely treed lawn on the square with fountains and flowers and a little walking path. She watched couples promenade along the cobblestones in the dark, some married and some, she suspected, not.

It wasn't her business although she would never do such a thing. Papa would boil over and lose his head. Mother had been noble in his eyes, with aristocratic grandparents, and he continued putting on such airs. She wrinkled her lips. Yes, his face would turn scarlet, and he would explode into his infamous temper and bellow until she covered her ears or the neighborhood heard.

"*Psst*!" The whispered hiss made her jump. Dolly Fenton, her closest friend and confidant stood on the top landing leaning so far over that she looked like she'd tip over. Her pumps made her look taller than her usual short and roundabout self, but she was familiar with the fashion catalogues from Paris and knew how to make herself look wonderfully adorable.

"Dolly!" Christine smiled with delight and held out her arms. "How I've missed you!"

Her friend darted down the hall and dove into her embrace. "You look divine," Dolly exclaimed.

Pushing her back, Christine examined her pinned curls, green gown, and dancing eyes. "Where did you get that necklace?" she asked with envy.

Dolly touched the painted locket floating from her smooth neck. "Papa gave it to me. For my birthday, remember? I wrote to you all about it. Do you even read my letters?"

"Of course, I do." Christine laughed. "I forgot, silly, and happy birthday again. I can't believe you're twenty-two now. You ancient thing!"

They both giggled, and Dolly squeezed in beside her on the window seat. They swung their legs back and forth in time and watched people dart up the stairs into the gaming room.

"I will always be older than you," Dolly said, "and you always half a year behind. But my goodness," she added, lowering her voice to a murmur, "I am so tired, Christine. Constance keeps me so busy with the children. There are three of them now. Can you believe it?" She wrinkled her pert, square nose.

Christine widened her eyes in agreement. "I shudder to think I'll one day have to wrangle the little devils, but really, four in six years, she must be exhausted."

Dolly nodded, her light brown curls bobbing. "Well, this will be number four, you're right, but she seems to enjoy them." She frowned like this was a great mystery.

"I might have had a little sister," Christine said and furrowed her brows, "after a little brother. Poor Prudence and the baby. I thought I'd die when they passed. She was like a mother to me. A second chance. Now I've lost Mother, dear James, and Prudence and that little boy. Poor me."

"She was a lovely stepmother," agreed Dolly. "I'm sorry you must live alone with your brother and Papa in that great house."

"It's not that great."

"Well, it's a fine house and almost as grand as the Blakemore's." Dolly gazed around the hall at the costly wallpaper. "True, you do not have a ballroom, but your family has restored your home since the war, and it's a lovely place unlike my poor abode in Charleston."

"Yes," agreed Christine. "I'm sorry for it. I'm sure someday it will be as good as new."

"Perhaps," murmured Dolly. "I hardly remember the revolution. It seems like a faraway dream."

"A nightmare." Christine frowned. "We were practically infants." She'd been sent away when the war began right after her mother's death. "Even in Darien I never felt safe."

At the other end of the hall, a gentleman burst out of the card room. He was trying to retie a cravat and doing a poor job of it. He tripped down the first stair and almost took a tumble. Both girls gasped and covered their mouths to giggle.

"He's already fishy tonight, I'd wager," announced Dolly, "and it's not even near dawn." She leaned back and gave a luxurious stretch. "We should go dance and dance together if there's no one willing tonight."

Christine patted her leg. "I heard they'll serve *macarons*." Just saying it made her mouth water. She did love a lick of sugar.

The door to the room where Matty had sought refuge jerked open. Christine caught herself gripping the edge of the window seat. She watched him dart out mumbling under his breath and heard the sharp chuckle of Captain Butler as he followed him out. The captain turned to shut the door and spied Christine a few paces away. For some reason, he stiffened then a slow, sideways smile spread across his face, and he winked. Dolly caught her breath, but Christine looked away and did not make a sound. Something about him made her pulse pound at her temples. The door clapped shut behind his back, and he followed Matty downstairs.

"What sort of a look was that?" Dolly wondered aloud, "and how dare he."

"Matty is hiding out from the dancing," said Christine, "and he's keeping questionable company."

"That's Mr. Butler, isn't it? Of Clearwater Plantation?"

"Yes," sniffed Christine, "that Clearwater family, although he goes by Captain Butler now."

"He is Mathew's friend?"

"Not that good a friend," insisted Christine, "or I would know of it. I think they were a little familiar before the war. Can you believe he looked me over like I was a *macaron* when we were introduced, and Matty didn't say a thing."

"Your brother keeps odd friends," said Dolly. "Handsome, but strange." She slid to her feet and held out her hands for Christine to follow suit.

"He's not any happier than I am to have Papa constantly badgering us to make advantageous acquaintanceships."

"Well, what is he doing with Captain Butler? Isn't it true his father went mad during the war?"

Christine raised a brow. "Something like that. Burned half the plantation house to the ground."

"Well, maybe their luck has turned," said Dolly with a lazy shrug. "At least he survived. Things seem to be improving for everyone now. I have two new gowns this season and my necklace, too."

"I'm happy for you," Christine said in a sincere tone. "Papa managed to hide away some money back then, and he's increased the family's holdings a great deal since, but it never seems to be enough." Christine wondered about Captain Butler's holdings. "Clearwater," she mumbled. "Where is that place? Not in town."

"Oh, no," said Dolly with a shake of her head. "It's south if I remember right. Not far from the waterways and swamps, you know."

Sudden images of thin, sharp grass and brackish inlet water flowered in Christine's head and with them, the distant figure of a man in high boots and no waistcoat. She nodded slowly as if she did know. She remembered now. She knew exactly who Captain Butler was, only she didn't know why he was lurking out in the marsh around her favorite inlet.

CHAPTER TWO

Nathaniel galloped his horse through the muggy night, veering toward the marshland to catch a gusty breeze. His head was fogged, but he didn't feel completely in his cups. A gnawing irritation kept him alert even though the moon was over its zenith.

The black thoroughbred he called Babram raced along, and Nathan kept his flintlock pistol gripped in his hand. The occasional errant might attack travelers in the swamps, and the roads along the marshes were not much safer. If not a disgruntled soldier or servant, there were snakes and alligators—the terrifying demons of the coastal forests.

Speaking of demons, he mused, there was Miss Christine Fryer to deal with. He knew her after a moment when she slipped into the room, but he did not put it together with the girl spying on him in the marsh. Not at first. Not until he stepped out into the hall and caught a glimpse of her a few steps back with that observant look on her face. Then it all came crashing down.

Mathew's little sister had grown since he'd seen her last. He wouldn't have taken notice of any Fryer daughters as a boy. He'd not become truly close with Mathew until the Revolution when they'd fought together aboard the same ship. Even after the war forced them to part ways, he'd been happy to return to

Savannah and find his good friend there, alive and without a British musket ball in his bones.

Although Nathan had never been invited to dine at the Fryer home, the irregular hunting trip, occasional card game, and drinks after hours at Clearwater, had renewed and secured the strong trust between them. Two years ago, Mathew had agreed to invest in Nathan's quiet little side business that avoided tariffs.

"By gads, don't get caught," he'd said with a shake of his head. He seemed more in fear of his father than officials.

The Butlers had owned a small, sleek fishing boat before the war. With just a few side trips unloading cargo deep inside the inlets before sailing into port, there was soon enough money to buy a real ship. Now Nathan had space and speed to sail down the coast to the Indies, trade lumber and goods, and return with sugar and molasses, sidestepping American charges on imports in Savannah. It wasn't piracy, not by his definition. With the British out of the way, the new government had wasted no time levying new tariffs on imports by '89.

Nathaniel shrugged it off. He'd done a little smuggling with his father long before King George's war exploded along the coast. It hadn't helped. When the plantation failed and Percy Butler lost his beloved second wife, he lost everything else, including his mind.

Just a boy at the time, Nathaniel escaped the madness and joined the Continental Navy. Now, after all of these challenging experiences, he meant to put them to good use and restore Clearwater to the way he remembered it. Smuggling was a means to an end until he could stand on his own two feet. He was an American soldier. He'd be a law-abiding American citizen... soon. The way he saw it, Fate and the sea owed him a thing or two.

He turned west at a rough fork in the road and slowed Babram as they passed the swampy woods southeast of the secluded inlet. When he reached the long sandy drive that led to his family home, a sense of satisfaction washed over him as he studied the lights in the windows.

Babram trotted with heavy breaths toward the house as Nathan examined the view. The four columns in the front house had been replaced. Banisters and spindles had been repaired on both the upper and lower porches. The roof was completely rebuilt, even where the flames from his father's fire had not reached. Fresh coats of paint made the house look like new. All of it in less than seven years.

Nathan allowed himself a small, bittersweet smile of pride as he rode up to the small stable. It'd all come at a cost. The rice fields had grown over. Workers his grandfather had used left once the laws forbidding slavery changed. Papa refused to purchase human beings, married the Creek woman, Laughing Sparrow, to the horror of Savannah society, and life as they knew it began to crumble away. Then the war came.

Babram whinnied in anticipation of a meal as Nathan dismounted outside the stable. Isaac was probably in the house, but he could put his own horse up. There wasn't much help around unless he hired out. Even the small friendly band of Indians nearby had abandoned them when the war moved south. It was then Clearwater fell into serious disrepair, and all they had to subsist upon was a little garden plot and a few animals.

Inside the stable, Nathan went in search of oats, his mind returning to those dark times. When Laughing Sparrow had fallen ill, his father's rages against the world and promises of revenge had turned to madness. Lost and nearly broken himself, Nathan had fled for battle. It was after that when Percy Butler sank deeper into madness and burned a quarter of the house down as Savannah was sieged. Then he'd hung himself. Nathan had returned home years later to tombstones and ashes.

As the night deepened, Nathan plodded into the house to change his clothes. Isaac was snoring in the back room beside the pantry. Nathan walked in and leaned against the door. The old smuggler was asleep with his boots on and a lantern burning low beside him. He rolled over in his sleep then sensed Nathan was there and jerked awake with a scowl.

Nathan grinned and whispered, "Sorry to wake you, old friend. I just wanted you to know there's nothing to worry about. The girl—the woman in the marsh—did not recognize us at all, and I doubt she'll report it since she was unchaperoned and far from home." He nodded at Isaac's look of doubt. "She's Mathew Fryer's sister, the merchant's daughter." He snorted then laughed. "Our partner's relative. I'm sure she won't say a thing."

NATHAN SLEPT INTO THE late morning before dragging himself to the study. He replied to a few letters of business then turned to his ledgers and puzzled over how to make his numbers add up. At dawn the next day, he packed his trunk and rode into town heading straight to the docks along the Savannah River.

His ship had sailed in two weeks ago, half-full of legitimate goods supplemented with Mathew's lumber. Business was done on River Street where he rented a small office in one of the warehouses and met with merchants and his purser, although he handled the accounting himself. Mathew kept his distance. His involvement did not need to be known. Mathew's business provided lumber to be shipped down to the Indies, but it also provided additional weight as unsold cargo to fill the space of the removed smuggled Caribbean goods when Nathan returned to port.

Nathan made the rounds up and down the row of warehouses then strode through the brisk salt air to his ship. Mr. Walker, his first mate, was the son of his father's old partner. He'd sailed the molasses triangle his entire life, and when Nathan had approached him to help him commandeer his own ship, he'd been keen on the opportunity.

"Tell me, Walker," he said, "are the men about and at the ready? I believe the weather is fair."

"The weather is fine, Captain," Walker reassured him. "I believe we'll reach the islands within three weeks."

"I want no new crew this trip," said Nathan. "We push our luck slinking into Savannah so light as often as we do now. It's profitable, but..."

"Yes," agreed Walker. The other two officers in the room remained silent. "Our legal business is well enough, but I do not trust all of the crew to keep quiet about our stops along the coast."

Nathan ran his fingers through his hair. "And we risk it so often these days. I just want a skeleton crew this voyage, those who have sailed under our black flag before, and who understand we'll unload in the inlet without any complaints or mentions to another breathing soul."

Walker clasped his hands on the table. "It's high pay and low risk. It should be no problem, even with Mr. Young nosing about asking questions."

Nathan lifted his gaze to the bulkhead. "Mr. Young?" The fat rat. "I should have never considered a loyalist turncoat who only joined our fight when the British left the coast."

Walker and the other men nodded their heads. The bosun said, "He ain't no better with numbers than he is rolling canvas, but he won't forget we didn't want him on board."

"God-willing he'll fall into the harbor and drown next time he's wandering around half-seas over," muttered Nathan. He was an honest crook by golly, but he couldn't stand a cowardly drunk. They set their affairs in order, and after a heavy dinner, cast off at low tide by moonlight to make their way out to sea.

Nathan felt good about the expedition. He would return a few days early and dodge into the inlet. There the crew could unload a portion of the cargo, and he'd continue on to the port the next day. Isaac would see that the goods made it to the plantation house and the cellar.

Nathan was close, so close, to finishing his work on the house and lining his pockets. Soon, he could get out of smuggling for good.

PAPA PERMITTED CHRISTINE to visit at Dolly's aunt and uncle's home a week after the ball, and to her delight, they were able to spend two days chatting and embroidering tiny caps and shifts for the baby on the way. The Fenton home sat on the northern end of town, not far from the river businesses, and after Christine's promise she would come again soon, she returned to her bleak and austere house on York Street.

She was unpacking her things and tidying up in her room when Abigail rapped on the door. "I came to empty your trunk," she said in winded words, "but Mr. Fryer has asked that you see him in the study."

So soon? thought Christine with a sigh. She surrendered to it with a forced smile, passed Abigail a shawl from last season and urged her to keep it, then took her time walking down the polished stairs watching the toes of her slippers move along at a snail's pace.

Sunshine beamed through the transom window over the front door, and Christine soaked in the cheerfulness before she reached the closed doors to Papa's kingdom. With a hard swallow, she ducked her head and knocked.

"Yes." It was not a question.

Christine forced herself not to roll her gaze up to the ceiling as she pushed the door open into the immaculate study. Papa sat upright in his chair with stacks of books before him and a cup of steaming tea placed to his right. Light spilled through the front windows and made the swords over the fireplace gleam.

"Hello, Papa."

Mr. Fryer leaned back in his chair. His wig was set aside, but new wiry spectacles were perched on his nose. "You're home, I see, and punctual as promised."

"I did agree I would return today. Mrs. Fenton is doing well."

"I'm happy to hear it," he replied with no expression. "I presume you recall we've been invited to dine with Hawthorne tomorrow."

Christine's heart plummeted to the floorboards. She'd pushed that obligation far from her mind.

Papa looked over the top of his glasses and raised his salt and pepper-colored brows. "I want you to bed early this evening," he ordered, "to get your rest. You were ill with the last invite, and I cannot have you decline another invitation from so precious and trusted a family friend."

Christine felt sick. "Yes, Papa," she murmured. Avoiding his gaze, she stared over his head at the rapiers on the wall. "Of course, I will be ready to attend."

"Very good," came the crisp response. When she dropped her studious gaze to meet his eyes, she saw he'd lost interest in her and had turned his attention back to an open ledger. "Wear your best," he added, "the apricot gown you last wore at Blakemore House. It's quite fetching."

Christine stared, waiting for him to look up. She didn't like that gown. It was cut so tight she had to cinch her bindings and so low she looked desperate for attention.

Papa's quill went into the inkwell, and he began to scratch again. Forgotten after his instructions as usual, Christine curtsied out of habit then left the room. Tears pricked under her eyelids. She made a beeline for the kitchen but finding flour in the air and herself in the way, slipped back upstairs to hide in her room.

MATTY VISITED AND SEEMED to scrutinize Christine during supper. He joined her later in the parlor as she sat alone with her thoughts and a pile of knitting. Papa had returned to his study after his conversation with her brother at the table.

She glanced up when he crept in but then returned to the yarn in her lap. He sat with a thump across from her, falling onto the settee and crossing one leg lazily over the other.

"What are you working on?"

She shrugged. "Mittens for winter this year. Papa does not want me knitting stockings like a working woman."

He snorted. "It's an honorable industry. I know several women who make a generous income with their craft, and it makes them less dependent on their husbands."

Christine barely looked up. "Yes, but Papa doesn't like it. He thinks it's unbecoming of me to make my own clothes now."

"Well, I admire your diligence. I hope there'll be a pair for me, too."

She glanced up at him to smile, but his gaze was focused on the low fire in the hearth. "How was business today for you?"

"The lumber business is thriving, and it's warm now. Of course, I ran errands for Papa since I was in town."

"Is that all? I thought I heard Abigail say you were down at the river."

Mathew look startled. "Well, yes, I was at the docks for a bit. Personal business."

"You have your ventures, I know. You're so fortunate, Matty, to have that charming cottage outside the city commons to live as you please."

Mathew seemed uneasy. He wasn't the oldest born son, but James had died and fate had dropped the family inheritance, responsibility, and future onto his shoulders—all under Papa's direction.

"I'm sorry you don't enjoy the family business, Matty," said Christine with a sad smile. She did not like being the only living daughter any more than he enjoyed being the only living son.

He shrugged. "It's not that. It's just I see a future in lumber and rice that's better than East Indian goods. Maybe even cotton if it could be pulled faster. There has to be a way," he mused. "There're other opportunities to make money outside of silk and china."

Christine raised a brow.

"I have my own ventures, as you said."

"I suppose that's why I overheard Papa complain your books are off-balance."

Matty shrugged. "Unlike him, I'm a poor bookkeeper. My shipping is irregular."

"Just what are you shipping then?"

He studied her. "Like I said, just my lumber and the like. I also invested money into Abe Shuttlecocks' business, and I have a vessel or two shipping other raw material to the Caribbean."

"Papa approves. He made a small investment in your company."

"He doesn't mind it," said Matty, "as long as he can examine my books and make more money." He said this with a wry tone, and Christine looked up.

"I suppose if you enjoy working with merchantmen and spending time on River Street, you should pursue it. It's certainly made the Blakemores a great deal of money.

"That it has," agreed Mathew. He shifted back into a retiring position, and Christine felt him examining her. "By the by," he said in a casual tone, "were you wandering in the marsh last month? South of town near Sandpiper Inlet?"

She looked up in surprise, but his lips pressed together as if forcing himself to look innocent. "Are you talking about your friend, Captain Butler?"

The cloud over Matty's face did not clear up. She knew he expected her to always be frank and was certain he was not speaking about anything else.

"Yes," he said after a pause. "It's just he mentioned it, you see, before he last departed for the Indies."

"He doesn't strike me as a ship's captain," said Christine with a shrug, "but yes, I was walking along the marsh looking for pink needlegrass, and I spied him in the distance. I didn't recognize him then, so I hurried away."

"Did you see him with someone?"

"Yes."

"Did you know him?"

Christine shook her head. "No, just a dirty, old sailor man I could have easily mistaken for a pirate."

"Did you hear anything?"

"No." Well, Christine paused in her mind. Had she heard something? It was their voices that had caught her attention, like the sound of hummingbird wings on the wind.

"My dear," said Matty, standing up to stretch. "You must forget all about it. You were practically out to Clearwater Plantation. You shouldn't wander out so far alone. Papa would be furious."

Christine nodded. "Yes," she agreed in a low tone, "but I know my way around with Janus, and Henry was busy in the stables. I'll be more careful not to go so far."

"Good," said Matty, "and don't go out to that inlet, not without me, understand? You don't want to run into some uncouth fisherman," he added.

She nodded, curious at his sudden concern about her hobbies, and irritated that Captain Butler had told him she'd been out riding alone.

"Actually, you should not go that way anymore at all—if Alligator George is having his way up and down the coast."

Christine said nothing. The rumors did not frighten her, and Matty was beginning to sound like Papa telling her what to do. "Busybody," she breathed, as Matty slipped out the parlor door. Then she remembered she had heard something that day. Why yes, Captain Butler had said something to the dirty sailor man that had ended with, "the next quarter moon."

CHAPTER THREE

M r. Hawthorne lived four blocks west and a brief jaunt north of the Fryers. Christine studied his home as the carriage approached, frowning at the ugly gargoyles perched on the rooftop corners. The sky looked overcast, and an earlier rain shower had not quite dried away. The streets looked muddy and smelled of damp, and the air felt heavy and sticky, a fore-warning of what summer had to offer when the coastal breezes died down.

Christine glanced down at her décolleté, white and dewy in the afternoon gloom, and when no one was looking, hitched up the sides of her bodice for more coverage. Her scalp hurt where Abigail had stabbed her with pins to keep her hair swept off her neck, and the attempt to curl her locks into pretty spi-rals was already failing because the heavy air tugged them back down.

The carriage clattered to a halt, and she waited for Papa to climb out. Another coach lingered across the street, and she re-membered with relief that they would not be the only guests. She didn't want to be alone with Papa and Mr. Hawthorne. She really did not.

With hands damp inside her gloves and her heart tripping like a clumsy colt, Christine stepped out. Someone had laid down a portion of canvas for her and other ladies to walk over to avoid the mud as they entered the house. Stomach clenched and chin up, she forced her legs to move into the house swirling with people and chatter. It was to be a small party Papa had said, but it already felt extravagant. She sighed under her breath.

After the usual introductions—there was no one Christine did not know—and an excess of attention from Mr. Hawthorne that made her cheeks roast from the knowing glances around them, the party moved into an opulent dining room with pewter candlesticks, fine china, and a table heaped with early greens.

Christine picked at her fish. She'd been seated three persons down from Mr. Hawthorne, and every few minutes he broke off his dull conversation with Papa and Mr. Shuttlecock and asked if she needed anything.

She could not force herself to speak so she shook her head every time. Papa's piercing stares made her feel even worse. Finally, the meal ended, and she hurried to join the other two ladies in the drawing room although they were far more her senior. Their leisure time ran short, and the gentlemen joined them too soon for Christine's liking.

Her heart nearly stopped beating when Mr. Hawthorne waddled across the room and took a position standing next to her chair. As the conversations about weather and commerce broke off into little groups, he leaned down and said with hot, liquored breath, "How lovely you look, Miss Fryer. Are you enjoying springtime this year? We haven't had too much rain and not too serious a storm, praise God."

Christine looked up and caught him peering straight down the top of her bodice. She put a hand over the lace to close up the view. "I'm grateful for the weather, Mr. Hawthorne. It's refreshing to enjoy the trees again without worrying about a cold."

His thin brows crinkled. She looked away with a smile plastered on her face. He had a fine dark green and gold cabinet she could study. It was a beautiful oriental design.

"Oh, my dear, it is far too chilly yet to spend too much time out of doors. You don't want to fall ill or be caught in poor weather."

She nodded because she could not disagree. Thankfully, someone stole his attention for a few lines, but he soon returned to her. His hand gripped the edge of her chair close to the back of her head and brushed her neck.

"My dear, Miss Fryer," he said, leaning down again like she was deaf. "Have you seen my new draperies from France? I must say even Mrs. Blakemore has admired them and so much so that she insisted she have her own."

"They're quite lovely," parroted Christine with a polite glance their direction. The blue damask shimmered in the room's light. The French were now engrossed in their own revolution, and she felt sorry for them as the discomfort of her childhood rose like shadows in the back of her mind. However he had lucked into them she did not know.

"I find them so," said Hawthorne, "quite lovely. Allow me to show you." A dry, spotted hand landed on her arm, and with a start, Christine found herself looking into his aging, eager face. He was not a horrible man, but he was as old as her father, and she could not think of him in any other way other than a friend.

She forced herself not to shudder at the foreign sensation of a stranger's hand touching her flesh. He gave a small tug, and she climbed to her feet and joined him. With a slight bow, he offered his arm, and they crossed the drawing room together to see the fabric and then wily as an old fox, Hawthorne led her from the room under the pretense of showing her a painting in the hall. In near panic, Christine looked back for Papa, but he only nodded at her with narrowed eyes and a look of satisfaction.

Down the hall and into a little alcove under the stairs, Mr. Hawthorne pointed out a piece of art he'd just purchased and fawned over the image of one of Savannah's beaches.

"I plan to have it hung in the drawing room when I can," he said in a proud tone. Voices from the drawing room drifted into the hall. "Not that this isn't a special occasion," he stuttered then touched her arm again. Christine pulled her shoulders back. In her pumps, she was as tall as he, just a smidge higher. Beside him with their arms locked at the elbows, he seemed to shrink in size.

She felt him gawking at her and concentrated on the painting. "It's very fine," she managed to say. She hoped she sounded courteous but not too impressed.

"I trust that you appreciate it, and I do hope I may show you the rest of the house the next time you come to visit."

Christine's breath caught in her throat. She tried to smile, but it would not come. "That would be kind," she said in a choked voice. She felt like she'd just swallowed mud.

The mollifying words had the opposite effect she'd hoped for, and Mr. Hawthorne beamed like a candle in front of a looking glass. He looked toward the drawing room and squeezed her elbow. To her concern, he then took her hand. "Miss Fryer—"

Christine felt herself sway. Whatever he was going to say, the anticipation of it made her feel hot and nauseous, and she did not want to hear it.

He raised a hand to steady her. "My dear," he said with concern.

"Oh, Mr. Hawthorne, I think I should return to my Papa."

"Why, yes, of course," he said in a rush. He looked ashamed he had done something to upset her. The gentleman escorted her back to the drawing room as Christine tried to ignore the cloying beats of her heart. As they approached the threshold, a breath away from escaping the most disquieting experience of her life, he stopped and whispered, "May I have the first dance this week next? Mr. Fryer tells me you will attend the ball at the Shuttlecocks in celebration of Mrs. Shuttlecock's birthday." She was so close to freedom she made a hasty nod.

Mr. Hawthorne's faded green eyes brightened under his brows. The wrinkles across his forehead disappeared.

"Thank you, my dear," he said, most pleased, and touched her arm again. "I do look forward to it."

Christine stared at the door until he pulled her through it, and they joined the others. She wanted to leap across the rug and throw herself behind Papa, but with all of the poise she could muster, she walked back to the hard chair by the fire and let the old man help her sit down.

TEARS STREAMED FROM her eyes and dripped into her hair that was splayed out across the pillow. Christine stared into the darkness searching for a crumb of comfort. Papa had been insufferable during the short carriage ride back. He'd talked of nothing but Hawthorne's house, Hawthorne's business, and especially Hawthorne's polite and attentive behavior toward her.

She wished nothing more than for Matty to come home, but she knew he would only repeat that Mr. Hawthorne was not the worst situation in the world. Her sullen behavior persisted into the next day of which she thought she would never escape. It rained, too damp to take a carriage ride, and Dolly could not come. There were no calls to make in such weather, nothing to be done, besides study the almanac or the bible or work on her embroidery.

By dinnertime and more of Papa's accolades for Hawthorne, Christine's patience had frayed to mere threads of self-control. Matty had made time to join them, but he mentioned the Shuttlecock's ball, and Papa declared with a steady gaze on Christine that Mr. Hawthorne would be there. She could not help but remember she had promised the man a dance. The constant worrying and implications made her almost ill. With an impatient snap, she tossed her spoon down and pushed back from the table.

Papa snapped, "Why Christine!" and Mathew's eyes widened, but she ignored them both and rushed from the room, dashed up the stairs, and slammed her bedroom door behind her. She allowed an angry cry that lasted only a few minutes before she climbed from the bed and washed her face. Changing early into her nightclothes, she slipped under the covers just as Abigail brought her a warm cup of chamomile tea. Christine drank it dutifully then burrowed down under the blanket wishing to be left alone forever. Sleep came, and she slumbered until the house fell still then woke suddenly in the middle of the night.

She had no idea what time it was, but she knew it was just another day closer to the ball. Dolly was eager to go, but Mrs. Fenton's time was near and perhaps she might not make it. That would leave Christine alone—with the daunting task of having the first dance with Mr. Hawthorne. The first dance. Everyone knew what that could mean. Perhaps none of the other young men would even dare ask her to dance afterward.

Tears moistened her eyes, but she forced them back. It was unfair. Her own family had fought for the freedom to rule themselves, and she was proud of them—proud of Papa's sacrifice and even James's although she could hardly remember him now. But where was her freedom?

She pictured the last time she'd seen her brother, James. His light brown hair had ruffled in the breeze as he told her goodbye. He wore a fine blue jacket over his golden waistcoat. A haversack crisscrossed his chest. There was the pair of new boots and sturdy tanned breeches. Papa had given him Ransom, their stud and best horse, and with a final dip of his cocked hat, James rode away with his boyhood friends, anxious to put his well-oiled musket to use. She never saw him again.

A thump in another room made Christine sit up with a sigh. She'd never fall back asleep now. She slipped out of bed and crept over to the window. The courtyard looked quiet, but who could tell. The dark night revealed little. Even the moon had waned into a dim but fat crescent, barely visible in the sky. May had brought warm weather. It was almost hot.

She pushed open the window and looked out. Movement below made her lean over. She caught a glimpse of a shadow leading a horse away and waited for the cloud cover to shift. Christine drew in a breath. She knew the silhouette and the horse. It was Matty and his mount, trotting into the night. He could not even wait until breakfast to escape his father and sister. They had argued in the study before supper.

Christine glanced at the sky. There was little enough illumination to see anything at all. Why would he go out? With a frown, she shut the window and stood in the middle of the room wavering in indecision.

Could she speak with Matty now? Be truthful and tell him she would rather live with him outside the safety of Savannah than marry an old widower? He had to understand. He was in no hurry to settle down, either.

She narrowed her eyes and felt around in the dark for the wardrobe. Pulling out her riding habit, she wriggled into it as best she could, tied up her skirts over a set of pantaloons and buttoned the matching jacket over her shift. With practiced quiet, she rubbed herself down with rosemary oil to ward off insects, picked up a cloak and her boots from the corner of the room, and then tiptoed down the back stairs wincing at every creak and groan. She thought of her brother's warnings not to wander, but he'd set off alone and in the tar pitch black of night. He was either abandoning her or up to something he wanted no one to know. Her instincts told her it was the latter.

"I'm mad," she muttered as she stealthily led Janus bareback down the side of the street as she'd seen Matty do. The hood of her cloak hid her face, but there was no disguising her horse. Curious but cooperative, Janus let her guide him to the first corner and then with a little help from a post, she clambered up and settled astride before starting off at gentle cantor in the direction that Matty had disappeared.

It did not take long to realize he was heading in a different direction than the city's commons. He'd set off southward, toward the little streams that led into the trees and then eventually, the wet, dark marsh. He'd told her to avoid the marsh. He'd insisted she not go out this way again. She thought of suspicious Captain Butler and then his words on the breeze. "The waxing moon," he'd said. She looked up at the night sky. Funny, Matty was heading out that way on such a night.

Christine chewed her lip under the hood as an owl hooted. Janus seemed to know exactly where he was going once he left the cobblestoned streets, but it didn't stop her from being uneasy. Although her eyes had adjusted to the gloom, she could hardly make out her hand in front of her face at times, and persistent insects buzzed around her in a cloud taking selfish bites if they could avoid her swats. As the earth gave way to grass, she worried about wild cats and alligators.

Alligators haunted the coast's waterways. They floated their way up the tributaries of Savannah's River. She'd seen a dead one once, and it was horrible and ugly with startling and enormous teeth. It looked like the dragons of her childhood nightmares. Christine suddenly understood the threat in the name of Alligator George and of his ship, *The Dragon*. He was a maneater.

Animal scurrying sounds, musical frogs, and drowsy bird calls made her twitch as perspiration trickled down her spine. Christine regretted her impulsive decision. What had made her act so reckless? Had curiosity won the best of her or was she jealous of Matty? Perhaps it was her anger at Papa for his relentless control of her life.

She had to admit a little part of her fancied the idea of running away into the night; of riding Janus all of the way to Spanish Florida to escape the droll routine of life on York Street. The war was over, and people were free. But not everyone was emancipated. She scowled. No, and not women, either.

A splash over the distant marsh made Christine jump. She pulled Janus to a halt to keep him from stepping into the unstable soil. It was dangerous for a horse. With a shudder, she prayed no monsters were watching her loiter on her prancing horse in the dark. A distant glow through the trees made her reign Janus in, and he snorted with impatience and tossed his head.

Had Mathew come this way or had he diverted down another path? Christine moved Janus forward another few steps until they were under the overhanging branches of a spindly tree. They both stared into the night. Bobbing lights moved over the marsh in an almost straight line. She waited for a cloud to pass over the moon to help her see through the shadows. Soft whispers came through the trees. She wasn't alone.

As shapes took form in the darkness, Christine realized it was boats out on the distant, shallow water. They looked small and light, just steady enough to maneuver up a small creek or stream and around a dank inlet. She'd have to cross the wetlands to get closer, but she couldn't risk it with Janus.

She studied the lanterns hanging in the boats and realized that the one pulled closest to shore was in the process of being unloaded. There seemed to be large men hoisting barrels and sacks onto their shoulders and disappearing into the trees.

Listening carefully, she assured herself they were not coming her way, although it would be the right direction if they were taking their cargo into town. She wondered why they did not continue up the coast into the mouth of the river. Her brows wrinkled. Why unload at Sandpiper Inlet?

Pirates? Her thudding heart began to race at the possibility that Alligator George was using this very inlet. There was sure to be a ship where the inlet became a waterway and opened into the sea. She remembered Captain Butler and his mysterious meeting that she'd stumbled upon. Christine narrowed her eyes with suspicion. Wait. Where was Matty after all? There was nothing around this inlet but marshy grasses, and further inland, Clearwater Plantation. Matty and his dubious friend were no pirates, that much was sure, so what did that leave?

Smuggling.

Christine drew in a sharp breath at the thought of Matty and his other "ventures." *Wicked Captain Butler*, she thought at once. He'd drawn her brother into a dangerous game.

MATHEW FRYER SPRAWLED out in one of the new club chairs recently purchased for Clearwater with a frown smudging his usually cheerful features.

"I assure you, no one in Savannah is the wiser." Nathan poured them both a drink.

"Except for my sister." Mathew scowled again. "She may have forgotten all about it by now, but if she were to hear the rumors..."

"Rumors?" Nathan tried to act unruffled and waved his hand. "Don't trouble yourself. There have always been rumors.

Before the war, during, and after. No one is the wiser. I'll creep into port tomorrow and unload the usual goods. If anyone asks, I'll tell them I dropped a load off in St. Augustine on my return, which I did and have the papers to prove it."

Mathew crossed his arms. "I'm sorry to doubt you, but I heard it mentioned at the tavern again. All it takes is one curious dodant asking questions before someone notices you seldom actually make your ports and that you do little trade when you are there."

"They can balance my books, and they won't find a thing. A few greased palms and no one pays attention to how much we carry out. You mustn't worry. Let Alligator George take the blame."

Mathew bit his lip. "That could be worse. Even my sister has spied you. Should you be caught, it would ruin my family, and yet here I am happily reaping rewards at everyone else's expense."

Nathan chuckled. "You should worry about yourself. It's your inheritance, and your father has no right to manage how you spend it."

"Well, it'd ruin my sister if I went to prison. There's no money for any of us if I'm sent there."

"I won't turn you in," Nathan promised him.

He'd made sure Mathew received a return on his initial investment, but he needed his friend's continued support to pay the crew until they ended things. Now would be the time to be completely honest, though. "I must tell you we did run into trouble north of Florida."

"What kind of trouble?

"A small brig flying our colors. I didn't want to be boarded and have an accounting taken so we outran them."

"Did they see your stern?" Matty's eyes widened, and he leaned forward.

"We have our disguise and were soon out of sight."

Mathew crooked his head in warning. "If you're caught you could hang."

"We're Americans now. At least they'd execute me here."

"Either way, the death of you would be the death of me," mumbled Mathew. He studied the cuckoo clock tick-tocking across the study.

Nathan wondered what Mathew thought about the recent changes. The wallpapers were colorful and bright. The Persian rug on the pine floorboards, thick and new.

"Our next trip, should you deem it safe, will probably be my last investment," said Mathew in the stalemate. "I'll stay and mention your companionship on a hunt or at cards, as usual, but I think I'll take the money I've won, and look for more legitimate avenues." He paused then looked Nathan in the eye. "I won't risk my family name as much as I want the income, and I won't gamble on your life."

Nathan nodded. "I understand. This will be my last year for it. Maybe it should be my last run, too. The crew isn't so happy, but no one wants to end up on the wrong end of the new Constitution. I'll branch out north, take in Plymouth perhaps, and become a completely legitimate shipping merchant." He twisted his lips into a look of regret. "It'll mean more time at sea and less time relaxing in the Caribbean, but at least I'll be set for life and the old Butler debts will be paid off in full."

"Clearwater will be yours once more, and you can join me regularly at the excruciating hunting grounds of Savannah's finest ladies."

"Oh, I'd sooner hang," joked Nathan. "I do hate a ball."

"Yes, but you see, you must immerse yourself into it little by little until you are numb, like the way one boils a frog." Mathew gave him a devilish grin.

With a frown, Nathan said, "I plan to attend the Shuttle-cocks' ball. I feel lucky to have received an invitation. You'll be there, I assume?"

"Yes, said Mathew with a roll of his gaze. "Papa will not turn down any invitation to strut his new wig, and he is anxious to see Christine off—to cut his expenses and responsibilities so he can enjoy his private life—whatever it may be."

Nathan raised a brow. "He may find the house lonely once you both are gone for good."

"No, it's what he wishes. He's never been a family man. He has more vices than the devil himself but hides them well. The only part of me he ever wants to see are my books."

"Well then," said Nathan, realizing he needed to get to his ship if he would make port tomorrow, "I should slog my way back through the marsh before it's too late. I'll see you at the warehouse then."

"Yes," said Mathew with an absent mind, "and the ball with Christine. She'll be dodging old man Hawthorne, and I'll be dragging her back into the ballroom time after time."

"Until then, old friend," said Nathan. They stood and shook hands, and Nathan patted him on the shoulder before releasing him out the door.

He returned to the study, satisfied. Hope washed over him. It wasn't what he'd planned, but could one more smuggling run to the Indies be enough to pay his final debts and set up the house? Could he end this chapter of his life and make it history? He put out the fire, gave instructions for the house to Isaac during his absence, and crept out into the night with a pistol at his side.

His thoughts swirled with details for the next day's fictitious arrival into port. Everyone seemed to believe his voyages were legitimate, and no one seemed to notice he made a few stops in and out of some of the waterways along the way.

He caught himself worrying his lip. It would be good to attend the Shuttlecock ball rather than skulk about at home and in the marsh until the next voyage. It'd let word pass he'd just arrived. He wondered if dancing with some of the desperate girls would make him appear more honorable—a poor planter's son who'd come into new money with his trading ship. Ha. Nathan was now richer than anyone knew—except for his wardroom and Mathew.

He hesitated mid-step and searched the constellation that would guide him back to the inlet and skiffs. *There. The she-bear.* His mind fluttered about like sea mist from the ball to dancing partners. Christine Fryer might be a safe companion, but no... She was too quizzical and sharp and watched him closely now. Not that he minded a beauty's examination, but there was no use getting in old Hawthorne's way.

CHAPTER FOUR

The Shuttlecock's ball was the fourth soiree since the season had arrived, but it was warmer now than the blustery, rainy days of April. The ball was not as crowded as the party at Blakemore House, which gave some relief, but the lovely home was just as lavish as the other abodes of the merchants and officials who'd taken up residence along Savannah's most prestigious streets.

Christine stood next to a warming stove, which was not in use, and pretended it was a potted plant. She edged close to it to hide herself but not so near as to smudge her overskirt and petticoats. Patting down her blue silk stomacher, she inhaled as she scanned the room looking for Dolly. She'd promised to come.

The musicians tuned their instruments, and the sounds made her wince. Her nerves felt as tight as fiddle strings, too. Why had she agreed to give Mr. Hawthorne the first dance? She'd spied his carriage upon her arrival but snuck away as soon as Papa was engaged in conversation with a wealthy planter. Dodging jacketed elbows and silk overskirts, she skulked around the ballroom staring at paintings and stopped at each window to examine the cornices like she was building her own home.

Mr. and Mrs. Shuttlecock entered the room, and she groaned as the crowds filed in behind them to watch the opening dance. She spied Mr. Hawthorne's tottering small frame and turned to look into the gardens again. A Talbot twin walked past the corner of her eye, and she followed his pleasing silhouette. Seth Talbot was a young fancy thing, quite the dandy, and he smiled and laughed, although he was never serious. His twin brother, Toby, skipped by, too, but Toby came to an abrupt stop to meet her stare. Christine grinned and gave a curtsey, and he took that as an invitation to speak with her.

"Miss Fryer," said Toby, "how well you look! I'm so happy to see you here. Did you know they will be playing All Fours later? Are you dancing tonight?"

Christine chuckled under her breath. "How many questions you ask, Mr. Talbot. Of course, I'm here to dance." She caught herself pressing her lips into a tight smile and made them relax. When the twins and she were very small, they had chased one another around their mothers' knees.

"Why then..." he said with a bow, but Papa and Mr. Hawthorne interrupted him, and Christine's heart sank.

"Why young Talbot," said Papa in his demeaning way, "you were off to join the militia, I thought?"

"Why, yes," said Toby, "but not until July. I'm going to celebrate the Independence Day in Boston with my aunt and uncle, and then I will be off to see great and wild frontiers with any luck.

"It's a noble career," said Mr. Hawthorne with a smile—but it was an aged and wise look, not an impressed or approving one. To Christine's consternation, he turned to her next: "Why Miss Fryer, you did promise me the first dance, did you not?"

Papa stared. Hawthorne beamed. Toby Talbot looked disappointed, and Christine cast her gaze to the floor to hide her reluctance. "Yes, sir," she managed to say, but it came out a squeak as the first dance was called.

He held out his hand, and she took it, brushing by Papa with a stoic expression. She would not pretend to be happy, but she would be polite. She was a Fryer after all.

She danced beside Hawthorne, who was as stiff as his starched collar, until her gaze met Matty's across the room. His eyes were filled with pity. To her surprise, Captain Butler stood beside him with arms hanging loose at his sides, his dark chin accentuated by his white cravat. Christine's stomach tied itself into a sudden knot, and she wondered with annoyance why her heart jumped into it, too.

The fraud. Here he was with her brother again. He looked completely innocent against the brightly-painted blue wall watching, but she knew what he was. Yes. She was almost sure.

Avoiding his examination so he could see what she'd learned, Christine forced herself to perform with Hawthorne's gaze rippling over her until the gentlemen on the floor made their bows. She smiled and thanked him kindly, but before he could escort her back into Papa's crushing presence, she melted into the throng.

Christine wound her way through the mass of bodies and found a small crowd in the drawing room. She settled on the edge of a vacant chaise lounge and pretended to straighten the lace hem of her sleeve. Dolly was nowhere in sight. Perhaps she was dancing with a Talbot twin. Across from her, two ladies spoke loudly from the settee.

"The *Black Heron* was accosted again!" said one in fearful agitation. "Can you believe it? Right under the nose of our very own privateers."

The other looked solemn. "I heard it was Alligator George, that dreadful American pirate."

"American," spat the other. "He's no right to call himself so. I heard he's a loyalist who didn't like the outcome of the war. Took to pirating instead of being punished for helping the Redcoats."

"Or hung," scowled her confidant.

Christine rubbed her nails and pretended not to listen.

"They need to put a bounty on the villain's head. We've had enough battle and bloodshed on our shores. To think it's only been almost a hundred years since Blackbeard was captured."

"Well, nearly that."

"He's a lunatic. As mad as Blackbeard, I dare say," the woman continued. "He'll get his in the end, mark my words."

Christine swallowed. Pirates were a dreadful thing, as terrible as, well, as smugglers. She deliberated when and if she should tell Matty what she had seen at the inlet on the nearly moonless night. Why had he gone out that way? She hadn't actually seen him on the shore, but...

The concern had been eating away at her peace of mind. If they would hang a pirate without question, there was no telling what they would do to a smuggler.

Toby Talbot wandered into the room and gave her a cheerful smirk. "Did I see you dancing with Hawthorne?" he teased.

She raised a brow with a warning look, hoping he would lower his voice. "He was the first to ask," she said with meaning.

"Well," said Toby with a shrug, "I did find a lovely partner. Miss Fenton, if you must know."

"Oh, is she here?" Christine jumped to her feet.

"She is, but she was asked to dance next by my brother, so she's losing her toes as we speak."

"I must go find her," Christine insisted. "Will you be staying late then?"

"Yes, but I'm allowed into cards tonight, did you know? I'd rather play cards than dance," he added then his cheeks colored, and he quickly apologized. "I'm sorry, Miss Fryer," he said, aghast at his confession.

"It's no trouble," she assured him. "Why I'd rather be doing a great many other things sometimes," she admitted, although she did like to dance with the right partner. Obviously, he would not ask her again even if he very nearly had.

Toby pointed down the hall. "Oh, look. Miss Fenton is just down that way, Miss Fryer."

One of the ladies on the settee crowed, "Mr. Talbot, I've just heard your news!" and he forgot Christine and trounced over to accept their congratulations for joining the state's militia.

Dismissed as she so often was by the easily distracted Talbot twin, Christine picked up her heavy skirts and returned to the large room set up for dancing. The fifers fifed and stringed instruments sang out their notes. It was almost as nice as the music of the marsh.

She allowed herself to admire the lovely glass chandelier shimmering in its own candlelight and decided it looked very well dangling over the bright sea of the room with its dipping and bobbing bodies. Voices murmured above the music and glasses of drink clinked from the corners.

The dancers divided themselves in the middle of the floor, splitting apart like the Red Sea, and Christine realized she stood centered in the front of the room and looked noticeable and alone. She turned to duck aside, but Hawthorne appeared beside her like magic, and she stumbled back in surprise.

"Mr. Hawthorne," she blurted, inching toward an empty chair against the wall. He grinned at her with teeth small and graying, and she thought she could almost cry.

"I thought you'd hurried home," he said with obvious pleasure that she was still about. "Are you ill?"

The thought she could feign an illness or some sort of attack crossed her mind, but she spied Dolly across the room in a bright lavender frock, standing in a circle of young men and admirers.

"Well, no," said Christine with a patient smile. "I'm only looking for my friend, you see."

"Ah," said Hawthorne gazing into her eyes. The next dance was announced, and the guests clapped lightly with pleasure. "See, Miss Dolly is going to dance," he noticed. "Let's show them how well we move together, Miss Fryer." He tried to be glib and fun, but it looked so feeble on his aged face that Christine felt sorry for him.

"Oh, I..." Two dances. It wasn't three, but what would people think? It would be so obvious and clear. Christine thought she would be sick. A heat on her cheeks began to burn. Hawthorne stared, his smile expectant.

She stuttered again. "I—"

"Miss Fryer?"

She spun about, her hopes raised at the new deep voice.

"Hawthorne, is it? I apologize. Pardon the interruption."

Christine blinked. Captain Butler was speaking over her shoulder to Hawthorne behind her, and her nose almost touched his chest. The faint smell of something musky and peppermint radiated from him, not a sour sweat or air of tobacco. It was delicious.

Delicious? Christine felt her eyes widen. Where had that come from?

"Miss Fryer?" Her gaze rose to his face, and she realized his lips were moving. "You did promise me this dance, did you not?"

Christine realized she was trapped between two men. She could feel Hawthorne watching her from behind because her neck burned with awareness. Inches away from her chin, Captain Butler inclined his head, and she realized he was waiting for a response.

"Oh, yes," she stammered, feeling half-witted and like a terrible liar.

He held out an arm, and she turned to Hawthorne. The apples of his cheeks had gone ruddy, but he didn't look angry. "I'm so sorry," she gushed, and a part of her was. "I completely forgot."

He nodded with a sympathetic frown. "You were looking for your friend. I understand." Then he gave her a faint, indulgent smile with a little bow.

"Do come now, Miss Fryer," said Captain Butler as the first notes of a country dance peeled out over the room.

She pasted a smile on her face and allowed the captain to walk her to the center of the floor. He was grinning knowingly—openly at her for playing his little game and fooling poor Mr. Hawthorne—but she was grateful and relieved.

Christine let her shoulders relax, but she remained on guard. When Captain Butler took her hands to lead her down the line, his touch felt like honey and fire, and she shot him a look of astonishment before jerking her gaze away. She no sooner regained her composure, and he said under his breath, "You owe me now, Miss Fryer."

She looked up in surprise, nearly tripping over her feet. As he escorted her to their new position, she muttered back, "I'm sure I do not."

Smiling and clapping, she tried to enjoy the dance, but Captain Butler kept grinning and staring. His attention unsettled her. Despite the reservations, she was not sorry he clung to her arm when it was over. A glance around the room told her Hawthorne was not in sight. Her senses told her to flee anyway, but the rest of her, curiously, wanted to stay.

Captain Butler directed her toward a tray of punch then led her over to a wall behind a line of spectators and the cold and unbusy stove. "You look thirsty. Take this."

She accepted the drink and shrank back behind the crowd, hoping Hawthorne would not find her again.

"Oh, don't worry about him," said Captain Butler, "he left the room patting his pockets. They are playing cards upstairs, just gentlemen and their purses, so you know what that means."

Trying not to look too relieved, Christine said, "I'm happy he can enjoy himself."

"Yes, he has plenty of money, doesn't he? But I'm sure he'd rather dance with you."

Offended at both of his comments, she met his eyes and frowned. His thick, slanted jaw was so jutting and male, it made her quiver a little. "I'm happy to dance with any gentleman at least one time," she hinted.

He chuckled. "Aren't we proper? I'll be sure not to trouble you again." She looked to see if he was serious, and he winked at her. "But I can't promise Hawthorne I won't." Christine tried to scowl. "Now," he said stepping nearer and lowering his tone, "I do believe you owe me something in exchange."

"I don't owe you anything, sir. Keep your affairs between yourself and Matty." Christine arched a brow then remembering who she was speaking to, added in a low tone, "And by the by, I would rather you not do business with my brother at all." She braced herself and gave him what she hoped was a threatening stare.

"Why, whatever do you mean?" Captain Butler's voice became deeper, and he narrowed his eyes.

Christine's heart began to patter in her chest. She was not afraid of him, not here, but she worried that what she suspected might be true. If it was, Matty was in trouble. "I couldn't possibly owe you anything," she repeated in a threatening tone, "because I saw you in the marsh." She glanced sideways to see if anyone was listening, but the music and stomping feet did not allow anyone's conversation to float very far.

Captain Butler's tanned face deepened to a shade of ruddy brown. He stared at her as if she'd threatened to shoot him in the face. Christine looked away.

"Why, Miss Fryer," he said in a whisper. He moved closer still, so close she could feel his breath on her ear. "I'm sure I have no idea what you're talking about."

She stared straight ahead, watching the dance but jerked her head up and down in a stiff nod that said, *Yes, you do.*

"I have no business in the marsh."

Christine glanced sideways at his lie. "Then why did I see you there? Twice now? And with boats and goods—and my brother." Without warning, the Captain's arm slipped through hers, and she felt the heat of his body as he pulled her against his side.

"Miss Fryer," he whispered in a warning tone, "whatever you saw, I'm sure you will forget it. It would be a great inconvenience to your brother and even to your family if you did not." His grip on her arm was firm, and Christine realized she was breathing so fast her bosom was heaving. Was he threatening her?

Captain Butler cleared his throat then turned to stand in front of her as if there was no one else in the room. He made a deep bow but leaned forward as he did so, so that his face almost brushed hers when he straightened up. Christine stepped back in surprise, sparks shooting down her spine.

"I apologize if there's been any confusion," he said with a sudden smile. His eyes glimmered with something else other than pleasantness. "Please let us forget about it." Captain Butler's smile widened, but the mask dropped, and he added in a low whisper, "Or I will ask you to dance again. And again. And again."

Christine's eyes widened.

"Or maybe I'll take you for a long turn, out of doors until we get lost. In the dark."

She stared in surprise as her mouth dropped open like a marionette's.

Captain Butler turned on his boot heel and glided away, leaving Christine frozen with fear and something else she couldn't define. Her body trembled all over from head to toe.

BLAST THE GIRL!

Nathan tried not to stomp across the ballroom floor or make eye contact with any of the wallflowers gazing solemnly from along the walls. A loud giggle made him glance over. Dolly Fenton and her throng of admirers were making jolly. He cursed the silly girl for not attending to her friend so that he did not have to rescue her from Hawthorne.

Why had he done it? He could have spoken to Miss Fryer later in private or let Mathew handle it as he said he would. It must have been something about her pleasing heart-shaped face and the way Hawthorne's attentions made the pink melt off of her cheeks until she looked as pale as snow. It'd pierced his heart.

Everyone knew Hawthorne had eyes for the pretty Fryer girl. There weren't many women in Savannah who shined as bright as their gowns; who did not cover their plainness with powders and rouges. She was an intelligent, serious girl, but in no way dowdy.

He admired her compassion, too, he admitted. Most girls would mock an old suitor like Hawthorne, but she was as kind and patient as her youthfulness would allow. Pity she did not stand up to her father, but she was certainly quick to protect her brother. She *had* seen too much. Did Mathew know?

"Captain Butler."

He turned, and Mrs. Blakemore swayed in front of him, her bust protruding and fair hands swinging at her sides. He'd almost made it up the stairs to cards but was now trapped between the stairs and the ballroom. Her deep-throated tone and its meaning smacked him in the chest, increasing his irritation at all of her kind and throwing a cloak of dread across his shoulders.

"Don't you look lovely, Mrs. Blakemore," he answered between gritted teeth.

She looked up at him with dark eyes through her dark lashes. "Thank you." It came out almost a whisper but seduction and invitation laced her voice. "I have not seen you in weeks," she said and gave him a pink-lipped pout. Before he could step back from the over-scented cloud billowing around her, she reached out and took his hand.

He glanced over his shoulder should anyone be coming down the stairs behind him. "I've been to the Leewards," he said. "We've just delivered our molasses, you know, as I'm sure your husband has received his order." He pretended to shake her hand then dropped it.

She gave a sharp lift of her chin, but she wasn't interested in molasses. "Well, we missed you," she said with a flirtatious smile. "I hoped to see you at the Talbots' dinner, but you did not come, and I was so bored." She made a pouting face again.

Nathan bit back his first thought, which was to tell her that her entertainment was her husband's duty. "I'm sorry you did not find it to your liking," he answered in a droll tone. His gaze flitted past her, and he pretended the hall behind her looked far more interesting. "I have little time for parties with my own ship to manage and the plantation to see to."

"Oh yes," said Mrs. Blakemore with a frown. "It does need a woman's touch, doesn't it."

She looked at him with meaning again, and the back of his heel found the first stair step behind him. "I suppose Clearwater will have to tolerate my maintenance and designs," he said in a firm tone.

He cut his eyes from her face and hurried up the staircase. It was rude of him, he knew, not to excuse himself or say good-bye, but she would never let him out of her claws unless he made a run for it. The last time he'd been cornered in a guest room where she'd complained openly about her regrets—that she had not bid him farewell when he'd left to fight, and how she'd been desperate for her family to survive.

Her shocking display had not moved him even then. She'd made her choice, and it had been to not wait on the likes of him. The Butlers had not been within the good graces of society before the war. He'd never been good enough for her then—handsome enough to flirt with and even let him steal a kiss, but then she'd cut him off—a young buck with a stung heart—and made fun of his family. Ladies did not settle for the gentlemen of Clearwater.

He certainly had no intention of letting Pricilla Blakemore salve her regrets with him now that she was prestigiously married and well-to-do—for at least a good dozen years now. Her husband did business with Mathew. Nathan would not ruin it for a fickle childhood sweetheart.

Scowling at the duplicity of feminine wiles, he stormed into the game room, and all heads looked up. "Gentlemen," he said with a forced grin, and they all nodded. Those with their heads in business instead of scandal knew he was no longer a young man in dire straits. They knew the master of Clearwater had money to spare—they just didn't know where it was from.

Two different tables invited him to join them, and he chose the one with Hawthorne and Blakemore. There was no one better to lose a few coins to and win their admiration.

CHRISTINE STOOD STIFFLY in dim candlelight staring into the looking glass as Abigail helped her undress. Her face looked wan and some of the pins in the back of her hair had come loose making her locks droop.

"Did you have a good time, Miss?"

"Yes, Abigail," agreed Christine.

She had enjoyed the second half of her evening. Dolly had come after all, and they stood at the front of the room cheering on the dancers when they did not have partners and whispered about Toby Talbot who'd asked Dolly to dance again right after his twin brother. Christine later complained in low tones about Hawthorne's attempt to wheedle a second dance from her, and Dolly whispered back she saw Captain Butler had chosen her to dance a reel.

"Everyone noticed." Dolly raised her brows. Christine nearly told her what he'd threatened in a wild and roguish manner but said nothing. She couldn't very well tell anyone she'd been sneaking out at night into the marsh. They'd think the worst.

Christine tried to push the flirtatious threats out of her mind, but they repeated in her head all night long like an annoying, chirping bird. It reminded her that he had a firm grip and a deep voice and wore a minty fragrance that made her hands and heart tingle. Despite the swirling feelings he brought on, all of his denials and his menacing behavior had made her deduce for certain that he and Mathew were up to something illegal in the marsh, and it had to be smuggling.

She frowned. "Miss Fenton was there," she said at last to Abigail's patient silence.

"I'm happy for you. I know you enjoy her company."

"I do," said Christine pushing down her unfastened petticoat. "We had a lovely time, and it will probably be the last fun for a while."

Her maidservant nodded wisely. "Mrs. Fenton is expecting soon. I know you're fond of her, too."

"And worried," added Christine handing over the bulky layer of silk.

"And Mr. Hawthorne, how did you find him?"

Christine heard the searching in Abigail's tone. She cleared her throat and turned to stare at her in the mirror. Rather than chide Abigail for her prying, she said, "He's well," but did not hide her irritation at her probing for gossip.

Christine wanted to scream that he was there and as old as ever, but she did not dare. Abigail brushed out her hair and said goodnight, and Christine climbed into bed. There was more moonlight now; much more than last week when she'd slunk through the near-dark to the marsh.

She studied the moonbeams, her fingers pulling on a loose piece of thread from her blanket. She did not dislike Mr. Hawthorne. It was only she felt nothing for him and was troubled by the large gap in years between them. She did not want to marry a man nearly as old as her father. Especially a man who'd already buried two wives. She shuddered.

Captain Butler's tall, broad shoulders erased the unpalatable image of her suitor. His attention to her had been both unwelcome and stirring. She'd been offered friendship and attention by several young men in recent years, but none of them had developed into the wild, sincere, and trustworthy love she imagined was just for story-telling.

Toby Talbot? She suspected Papa made every effort to steer him away. The twins were fickle young men with their good looks and could have any young lady's heart they wanted, but neither were in a mind to marry.

And Captain Butler? The mysterious captain was around Matty's age, she guessed. He had warm hands, large and bear-like, that she suspected were as rough as the rest of him underneath his fine cravat.

Frustrated with his appealing qualities, she flopped over onto her back with a huff. How dare he threaten her under his breath. He'd even hinted he would ruin her for questioning his suspicious activities. She frowned and glanced toward the window. There would be no more trips to the marsh, she decided. At least not Sandpiper Inlet. She hoped never to see Captain Butler so intimately again, and she would certainly never accept another invitation from him to dance.

CHAPTER FIVE

Nathan had called on Mathew once before, but it'd been almost two years ago, and the elder Fryer's coolness made it clear there would only be business between Fryers and Butlers and nothing more. Instead, Mathew and he chatted at the docks or met in the River Street taverns. Sometimes, Matty rode out to Clearwater, but they didn't display their brotherhood too openly with the smuggling operations underway. He had no choice today.

With a deep breath, Nathan mounted the stone stairs two at a time and rapped on the door of the Fryer's home. A young woman in striped cotton and an apron answered the door. When he asked for Mathew, she let him in but left him standing in the hall. He walked closer to the open parlor door and studied the large portrait over the mantel. It was of a beautiful woman holding a handsome child. The first Mrs. Fryer, he guessed. Miss Fryer favored her, although she was not as thin and fragile-looking. Miss Christine Fryer could hold her own, that much was clear, and she wasn't a bad horsewoman, either.

A sudden movement caught him by surprise, and he realized Miss Fryer was sitting in the corner of the room watching him. She wouldn't have been expecting him. Her wide-eyed astonishment almost amused him, but the shape of her small, round eyes and the cupid's bow over her rosy lips caused a rolling wave of warmth to spread across his chest, and it surprised him back.

"Butler!"

He turned with a start and found Mathew on the walnut staircase looking at him in surprise. Questions swirled in his eyes, but Nathan pretended not to see them. "Mr. Fryer," he said in a cordial voice, aware of the servants—and Miss Fryer—listening from all parts of the house.

"You've come about the lumber shipment, I suppose?" said Mathew in a tense voice.

Nathan forced a nonchalant smile. "Yes, I'm sorry to call unannounced, but I had questions about our next shipment, and you were not at your cottage in the commons." He tried to sound innocent, but Mathew would know exactly what the next shipment was all about.

He gave a dip of his chin and motioned for Nathan to follow him upstairs. They no sooner closed the door behind them, then Mathew dashed across the room to check the back of the house for servants loitering about. He closed the window then turned and sat on the sill's edge so he could see into the courtyard and still converse.

Nathan dropped uninvited into a dark green chair. It stood out against the bright white-washed walls and the colorful paintings of farms and ancestors.

"You did not lose much in the war."

Mathew shrugged. "The house was occupied by a British captain. With Christine sent down to Darien, the servants were moved out to a farm under house arrest, but nothing of value survived."

"It's looking proper after all these years," said Nathan kindly. He swallowed a prick of indignation toward his father for trying to burn Clearwater to the ground. The old fool had decided to take it to the devil rather than see a loyalist in it. He shook his head to clear it. "I need to be certain of your next shipment to the warehouse. I can load the lumber on Tuesday next."

Mathew glanced out the window and said in a hushed tone, "Tuesday then and I will have my secondary shipment delivered to Clearwater Plantation."

Nathan smiled. "Yes," he said, "for *construction*," although the lumber would really be loaded onto his ship later, unaccounted for, and shipped to the Indies to sell to a contact who bypassed tariffs.

"This is the last time," Mathew said.

"Yes, I understand." The revenue would benefit them both, but Nathan would turn his profit right back over to his moneylenders to pay off the last of the plantation's repairs. "I will be free and clear," said Nathan with a sigh.

Mathew understood. The last smuggling voyage would have nothing to do with the Fryers. It would be Nathan's last secret maneuvering, and he would end the Clearwater smuggling legacy forever.

"But that is not why I came." A tremor pinched his chest, and he leaned forward. "I'm afraid we may have a problem."

"Someone is asking questions at the docks?"

"It feels like some are watching, but no, it concerns your sister."

Mathew grinned. "You saved her from a second dance with Hawthorne, but I don't think she's prone to feel indebted to you."

"No," agreed Nathan, "and she doesn't appear to like me at all, but there is something you must know."

Mathew tensed.

"She warned me at the ball to stay away from you. I believe she knows—everything—although I don't know how."

"She's perceptive," admitted Mathew, "and can be quite nosey." He sighed. "Ever since our mother died, she's clung to me and shadowed my every step. And she's not fond of our father. They are not close."

"That's not uncommon," said Nathan, brushing it away, "but following you into the night does seem to be a frequent occurrence." He gave Mathew a telling stare.

"What do you mean?"

"I mean she claims she followed you to the marsh the last time you were there."

Mathew's mouth dropped open. He caught himself and whispered, "In the middle of the night?"

Nathan pressed his mouth into a grim line. "I don't know how, but she saw everything."

"I did dine with them that night and take my old room here, but... You're sure?"

"Yes, she threatened me. She warned me to leave you out of my business, or she'll report my suspicious activities at the inlet."

"I can't believe it." Mathew looked dumbfounded.

"I'm afraid I was harsh. I admitted to nothing, but I told her I'd ruin you, her, and your family name, too, if she breathed a word."

Matty slumped his shoulders and fell back against the window's frame. He wiped his forehead with a palm. "I can't believe she would sneak out at night like a common—"

"Smuggler?"

A rap on the door left the words hanging in the air. Nathan's heart lurched in his chest. Had someone been just outside of it listening? He drew in a sharp breath and resettled himself in the chair so that he looked like he'd been sitting comfortably for some time. Mathew raised the window a crack and moved over to the chair across from him. "Come in," he said in a sharp tone.

The door opened, and Nathan felt relieved and annoyed at the same time. Miss Fryer was holding a tea tray that looked harmless enough, but her dark gray eyes were stormy and her jaws clenched.

"Christine." Mathew didn't try to hide his relief. He motioned for her to come in. She strode forward and nudged the door shut with a slippered foot. Nathan remembered himself and jumped to his feet.

"Miss Fryer."

She clapped the tray down on a three-legged table beside Mathew's chair and pierced Nathan with a sharp look before turning to her brother. "What is he doing here?"

"What do you mean?"

Miss Fryer gave her brother a matronly stare. "You know exactly what I mean. He's—" she stopped and folded her arms across her petite frame. "I know you do business with him, and then again, I know you do *business* with him."

Mathew remained silent. Miss Fryer leaned forward. "He's. A. Smuggler." She said it in a loud hiss then rocked back on her heels. Fear and a smug look of satisfaction mingled on her features.

Mathew swallowed so loud Nathan heard it in the silence of the room. He watched brother and sister stare at one another then slumped back into his seat with a sigh.

"Well, Miss Fryer, I suggest you sit down."

"No." She swung back to him and glared at him with blazing eyes. "I know you're up to something dangerous and wrong."

"It's harmless," said Mathew in a sudden rush.

She ignored her brother and shook her finger at Nathan. "I told you to stay away from Matty, to leave him out of whatever you're doing sneaking around that inlet with your crew in the dark."

"It wasn't my crew," lied Nathan with a lazy shrug. "As I told you at the ball, you have no idea what you saw, and it's best you forget about it."

The glowering little biddy balled her fists at her sides. "You're smuggling," she said in a threatening tone. "It's illegal now."

"Is it?" Nathan couldn't resist teasing her. She looked so self-righteous and assured, he added, "Maybe you just spied Alligator George."

"Then I'll go fetch my papa right now."

"Christine," Mathew blurted again. He took her hand and guided her into the chair he'd taken at her abrupt arrival. "Please. Sit down."

She allowed him to seat her, but when she looked up, she frowned at Nathan across from her. A horse nickered in the courtyard, the only sound to permeate the silence of the room.

"You know I am anxious to build a place of my own," Mathew began.

She nodded curtly.

"I'm seeing the parcel of land I purchased west of town cleared, and Captain Butler is shipping out the lumber and making the sales for me."

"And bypassing any tariffs." She was too clever for her own good, the minx. She looked up into Mathew's eyes. "Or something like it, Matty. Tell me you did not know. Tell me why you rode out to the inlet earlier this month."

He frowned, his brows nearly touching his eyes. "What were you doing following me in the middle of the night?"

"I was concerned about you." She flushed. "I couldn't sleep, and I heard you get up so I followed you out, but only to talk. Then you went the wrong way, toward the marsh, and I followed you until I lost you at the inlet—and," she pointed at Nathan, and he jerked back like she'd actually poked him—"his men were there unloading barrels and things in the middle of the night."

"How do you know they were my men?" asked Nathan innocently.

Miss Fryer gave him an icy gaze.

"He's doing me a favor," said Mathew. He glanced at Nathan. "You're right, Christine, I'm trying to make as much out of my investment as I can." Mathew sighed, wiped his brow, and walked over to look out the window. Her eyes followed him, but Nathan could not quit staring at the petulant, furious sister.

She was taller than most women, and confident and assured, despite her father's well-known low opinion of them. He was wrong about this one, Nathan suspected. She caught him studying her, and he held her gaze until she looked away. He could swear her cheeks flushed.

"What investment?" Curiosity got the best of the kitten. Nathan felt a grin twitch his lips, and she glanced at him and glowered.

"My inheritance," explained Mathew. He folded his arms and moved back to the window. "I'm seeing to the lumber sales from my parcel of land and investing in Captain Butler's... business. Soon, I'll have enough to build a fine house, maybe even have a plantation, too."

Her face paled in fear. "You would leave Savannah for good?" She threw up her hands, and Nathan thought she would jump to her feet and throw herself into Mathew's arms. "Why do you need to leave now? You're not married, you have that pleasant cottage outside of town, and I am here."

"But you forget," interrupted Nathan, unable to resist. He gave her a wide grin. "You won't be here for long if Mr. Hawthorne has his way."

She scowled back at him. "You stay out of this."

"Let your brother go."

"This is none of your business, Captain Butler, and as far as I'm concerned, my brother has no business doing business with you."

"You must stay out of it, Christine," said Mathew in an urgent whisper. "This is the last time, I promise."

"What's the last time?"

"Nothing," said Nathan and Mathew together.

Nathan could not have her interfering anymore. Surely, she did not know the date of the next shipment.

She gave Mathew a hard stare. "There will be no more times then. You're through."

"Yes," fibbed Nathan easily because he suspected Mathew could not. "We're just settling our affairs." Miss Fryer's shoulders folded with relief, but Mathew said, "No. I have one more shipment to go out through Clearwater Plantation. Captain Butler will take care of it for me, and then we're through."

"We were in the clear, my friend," said Nathan in frustration.

Mathew shrugged. "She should know. I don't want her following me anymore." He raised his voice and cut her with a steely gaze. Miss Fryer lowered her head. Would the chit surrender now? Keep quiet?

"Do as your brother says," said Nathan in a warning tone. He didn't care how she rumpled his emotions. He could not let his admiration for her cloud his judgment.

"Do you promise?" Miss Fryer studied her brother with concern etched onto her now tender features.

"One more trip," Mathew assured her, "and I won't even be aboard."

"Keep quiet about it, if you please." Nathan used his hardest voice. Rather than appear intimidated, Miss Fryer turned on him, and her features transformed from angelic to bewitching. "I'm not your business partner, Captain Butler, you don't tell me what to do."

He gave her a hard stare to remind her of their private conversation at the Shuttlecock's ball, and she stood abruptly and stormed from the room.

CHAPTER SIX

D olly's aunt had her child, a healthy baby boy, and summer snuck in so that it was not only warm but also dull without Dolly's company. Christine escaped to the treed lawn in the center of the square with Abigail on a late and stuffy afternoon.

When her stomach rumbled for tea and biscuits, she urged Abigail to match her pace as she hurried back home. Mathew had been away several nights in a row, staying in his own quarters outside of town, and when she'd asked Papa about it, he brushed it off saying in no uncertain terms to mind her own affairs. Perhaps Mathew was seeing to his lumber, but Christine secretly worried he might skulk away to Clearwater for another transaction for his "investment."

As she drew near the house, Christine saw a carriage idling there and wondered if it were the neighbors or if Papa had a visitor. She did not object to his friends if they kept out of her parlor and away from the dinner table. None of them had a mind to offer a young woman any attention anyway, at least not the married ones.

She found their conversations about loans, debt, and money dull, and could not bear the dreadful reminiscing of the war. She would never forget it and didn't want to be reminded that others had endured worse than she.

With the cheerful thought of tea, she burst into the house laughing at the crooked angle of her parasol and Abigail's promises to bring tea to the parlor if she did not faint from the rush in the heat. A flurry of voices drifted from the study, and when Christine looked, her heart sank as Mr. Hawthorne stepped out with Papa grinning behind him.

The carriage. She should have recognized it. Hawthorne's horses always sported ridiculous ostrich feathers in their manes that were better suited for a lady to wear. Lowering her gaze, Christine waited for the inevitable.

"Miss Fryer," came his kind and soft voice. She curtsied. His hand was outstretched, and she had to meet it. "I hoped I would see you today."

She grimaced and hoped it looked like a smile.

"Mr. Hawthorne has come to call," said Papa in a jovial voice that sounded pretend.

"I see, Papa. I'm happy I was not here to bother your business meeting."

"Oh, no," Hawthorne assured her. His eyes crinkled around the corners. "I came to call on you, Miss Fryer."

Christine's stomach sank like a stone. Papa chuckled. She glanced at him and saw warnings in his stare. She must accept Hawthorne's attention, or he'd be insulted.

"Mr. Hawthorne and I have had our meeting, but it was only on account of missing you," her papa informed her.

Christine waved over her shoulder. "It was so nice after the rain and not too sultry that I thought I'd take a turn about the square."

"Well, yes and here you are, safe and sound and lovely, my dear." Hawthorne's paternal compliment left her speechless.

Christine lowered her eyes. "But I cannot stay," he apologized, and her heart surged with quiet relief. "I have another appointment at the warehouse."

"Yes," said Papa, brushing past Christine like she was no longer there. "You will have a word with Mr. Gabble, will you not?"

Hawthorne turned to Papa and nodded. "I'm sorry that the books are not in good order. Perhaps your son has lost some papers, but don't worry, Mr. Gabble is the best man to get it straightened out."

Papa gave Hawthorne a tight smile, but a fist of panic jabbed Christine in the chest.

"He's a clever young man, my Mathew, but he refuses to use my bookkeeper. I'll speak with Gabble and seek his advice."

The older man nodded, and his watery gaze returned to Christine. "I am sorry to miss your company, Miss Fryer," he repeated. "May I ask you to dine on Friday? You will be my very special guest." He glanced at Papa, and Christine's stomach curdled like hot milk.

"Of course she will," said Papa, and he gave Mr. Hawthorne a deep bow followed by a handshake. When the door shut behind him, Papa gave her a stern look.

Christine twiddled her hat ribbons in her fingers. "What's wrong with Matty's accounts, Papa?"

"Your brother has made a great deal of money," he replied in a proud tone. "Hawthorne is only trying to help right the books. He has a fine accountant he shares with Mr. Gabble."

She stared, her mind whirling with images of ledgers and the smugglers in the marsh. He waved her off. "It's nothing for you to fret about, Christine. Go upstairs and take your rest. We shall have a serious discussion this evening, you and I, and I'll deal with your brother and his accounts when he returns."

THE "DISCUSSION" WAS worse than she'd expected. Papa spoke, and she listened, all through the evening meal and afterward in the parlor. He reminded her of her good mother and all that she'd accomplished in her short life. Then he reminded Christine of her duty as a daughter and as a Christian woman to herself and to the family name.

"Mr. Hawthorne is in want of a wife," he said with a meaningful stare, "and you have made little effort to seek a husband now that you are grown.

"I'm not yet two and twenty," she managed to say, but he ignored her after listing many of her peers who were rearing children before they were twenty years old. Shamefaced at his censure, she stared at a flickering candle in its chamberstick until he left her to smoke in his study. As soon as she could escape, she hurried upstairs.

At nightfall, on top of her mother's quilt in the oppressive darkness, Christine's heart roiled with a hundred fears. Papa was close to learning about Matty's smuggling "investment," and Mr. Hawthorne behaved as if he might propose. The crushing blows made her chest feel like a wagon had rolled over it. If she did not speak with Matty before Papa they would all be in trouble. And what of Hawthorne? She could hardly sleep.

At dawn, Christine dressed as swiftly as she could after eating very little. Papa went to River Street on most mornings, and she was anxious to go with him and have a word with her brother. Surprising Papa downstairs, she stayed quiet on the short carriage ride to the warehouses, her teeth rattling as they bounced over the cobblestones.

Papa stopped at the Fryer warehouse stuffed with goods waiting to be traded or shipped north, and ordered her to follow him in a brusque tone. Clutching the brim of her finest bergère, she stepped out and kept her demure gaze to the ground as she followed him inside the building. The clatter of horseshoes and wagon wheels echoed from the cobblestones over the lapping waves and hoarse voices of seamen calling good morning. The air smelled salty and sweet over the stench of animals and tar, and she could hardly believe the sea was so many miles away. Gulls cackled overhead, their irritating cries splitting the air.

When Papa was distracted with his inventory, Christine melted backward into the bustle of bodies going in and out of the door of the brick warehouse and disappeared into the street. Keeping close to the row of buildings, she hurried north to the head of the port where she suspected Matty would be with his foreman.

He had veered away from furs and leather and found a profitable market in the trade of lumber, but she had to be certain he was no longer in business with the smuggler at Clearwater. Just thinking of Captain Butler should have made her angry, but her innards shrank with worry, and her heart skipped a beat.

Annoyed, Christine strode past ogling men and vessels and warehouses, praying Mr. Hawthorne would not be about. Matty sent his lumber to a warehouse on the outside end of this port. She hurried toward the slips and pilings where he often stopped to converse with friends and sea captains. An important-looking man on the dock watched her approach, and by the deference shown him by the other sailors around, she assumed he was an officer of the Charleston-bound schooner readying to leave for the mouth of the river.

Moistening her lips, Christine pasted on her brightest smile. "Good morning. I'm looking for my brother, Mr. Mathew Fryer. Have you seen him about?"

The man removed his cap and with a slight bow said, "I have not since yesterday. We have some of your father's goods on board, but we will not set off downriver until the tide is agreeable."

"I see." Christine nibbled her lip, thinking. "I don't suppose you know where he meant to go next, do you?"

The gentleman stared, his raised brow telling her it was not her business what her brother or any man was up to. She realized her error, and that he might think Matty up to something less than honorable if his family did not know his whereabouts. She felt her lip curl and almost defended him outright. Matty did not keep a mistress, she thought with disdain, but the odd knowing look on the captain annoyed her.

"Thank you," she said in a crisp tone, and then, "I don't suppose that you have seen Captain Butler?"

The man looked quite annoyed with her now. "I don't know the gentleman's business, but I do know his ship, the *Siren*, set sail down the river just this morning."

Christine looked across the river, her mind estimating how long it would take a light ship to reach the outer banks of Savannah and stop for additional cargo in the swamps. She frowned. "Thank you, sir," she said with a curtsy.

He touched his forehead in an odd salute as she turned away with a mind hurtling possibilities in every direction. Matty was probably at Clearwater. Her worst fear. Should Papa find out, or Mr. Hawthorne, or the officials...

She should not have spoken to anyone along the river. Christine trembled at what she had done, and with a tight chest, stumbled back onto the street, jerking in fear when a fist grabbed her shoulder and spun her about.

"What are you doing here? And alone?" Papa sounded like he might burst. "I've been looking up and down the streets for you! I thought you'd been snatched and stowed below a deck."

Feeling her face pale, Christine tried to chuckle, but his face looked red as beets, and his eyes were wide and glaring. "I'm sorry, Papa," she stuttered. "I was looking for Matty." The truth was better than anything at this point.

Papa took her elbow in a pinching grip and forced Christine back across the street into the shade of the tall warehouses. They marched toward the distant carriage, and she was grateful for the distraction of the busy crowd. Lifting her petticoats over puddles and trying to calm her heart, she kept her lips closed tight and her thoughts to herself.

Papa invaded them as he pushed her up into the carriage. "Your brother is a grown man, Christine," he said in a stiff tone, "you will not worry about him anymore."

"Yes, Papa," she quickly responded. It was almost as if he was relieved Mathew had made a modest fortune and planned to leave them for the rough country west of town.

Feeling damp between her layers, Christine exhaled with fatigue as the carriage moved away from the cool breezes of the river. He was certainly eager to be rid of them both and have the house all to himself. She thought about the lovely Hawthorne home, but it did not cheer her up at all. What did anything matter if Matty was charged with smuggling?

She kept to the parlor for the rest of the day, pretending everything was fine and working with her tambour frame on a petticoat hem as if she was anxious to fill her dowry chest. Instead, she was thinking furiously about how to get into Mathew's room and see if he'd left a clue.

AFTER SAYING GOODBYE to Mathew, Nathan closed the door and stood at the window watching his friend canter away into the night. Mathew would return to the small house he had leased outside of Savannah's limits when he took it upon himself to oversee the production of lumber.

The near ton of pine and other wood would be the last shipment from Mathew to bypass the port and officials. Nathan would have no problem selling it in the Indies. Their tariffs and taxes were easy to avoid if one knew the right smugglers.

He returned to his table and put out the single glowing candle. He'd made sure the few servants he had were out or preoccupied—most of them would not realize he was home. The others, they would never answer if there were questions. Loyalties to the farms and rice plantations in the backwoods were different than among the wealthy of Savannah. No one should suspect he'd returned home by way of the waterways since leaving Savannah. No one would be the wiser.

Throwing a sack over his shoulder, Nathan slipped out the kitchen's back door. It was not a bright night, but clear enough for the stars to light the way as his eyes adjusted to the darkness.

Crickets cried and frogs belched while the ever-present mosquitoes flitted through the air making buzzing sounds in his ears. He plodded through the heavy foliage along the property's fence until it joined a footpath near a brook. It would continue until the ground grew thick and mushy and then with his pistol at the ready to warn off wild cats or other vermin, Nathan would hurry the rest of the way to the inlet.

Time seemed to stand still as the tree branches overhead made skeletal pictures in the gloom. The occasional hooting owl made his ears prick up. These sounds he knew—had known—since his boyhood. The music of the marsh was layered deep in his bones. It was the quiet that unnerved him.

When he was just a few yards alee of the inlet, he thought he heard the murmur of voices on the intermittent breeze and suspected the crew was loading the rest of the goods he'd stored in the cellar. They would row down to the *Siren* which waited in the depths of a waterway that led to the sea. Nathan licked his lips in anticipation but bit down when a shadow came at him out of the darkness.

"Captain?"

Nathan jumped back, pulled his pistol, and let a mild oath slip out. It was Isaac. The long-bearded man acting as lookout made a choking sound like he was trying not to laugh. Nathan stuck the pistol back in his belt. He moved into the clearing where he could make out the outlines of his men and their small vessels in the distance. "What is it?"

Isaac motioned north with his head in the dark. "There's someone or something moving about in the grove of cotton-wood trees. It could be a fox—or a man."

Fear and anxiety turned Nathan's heart to cold marble. Not tonight. Of all nights. He needed to get away, to unload this last shipment and pay off his debts. His final smuggling expedition should have gone unnoticed. There would be no more stops at Clearwater coming and going the next time. It would be the start of his legitimate shipping ventures.

He brushed past Isaac and crept through the trees, squinting in the darkness and holding his breath to listen. As his boots found their way through the sopping grass, he stopped just short of rounding the head of the inlet.

There! In the trees, a flash of white and silver in the darkness. He froze, his hand moving to his weapon again. Was it a spy? Someone from the port? Surely not.

Locking his jaw in frustration, Nathan moved without a sound through the trees to come around and catch the intruder in the act. His heart thudded with dread. He could not risk being exposed now. He was so close—to wealth, success, and saving his family name. But what if it was someone investigating from the docks? A nosy official like Mr. Young or a soldier from the militia? Was he really prepared to kill a man and become what he'd only pretended to be?

SHE WAS UNSURE OF THE way to Clearwater Plantation, but Christine knew her way to the marsh. Trembling, she pressed up against the warm, rough bark of a tree and stared out over the wet grassland. Her eyes followed the distant bobbing lights she knew by now were men and boats leaving the winding waterways. The only problem was, she had no way to be sure if it was Captain Butler and his sneaky men. She'd only ever seen him with one skiff before. And Alligator George haunted this coast, too.

She swatted at a pesky bug humming around her throat. Sweat dribbled down the back of her knees. It was insufferably hot. Summer had the countryside in her heavy, thick grip.

A crackling in the bushes nearby made Christine jump, and her breath caught in her throat. It sounded like someone had kicked a stone. She stumbled deeper toward the cover of the thicket to hide, but a wide, hot hand went over her mouth, and she released a muffled scream in terrorized response.

"Hush," a deep voice whispered, and her arms rippled with goose-skin. Christine wheezed against the hand to catch her breath. If these men belonged to Captain Butler, they wouldn't dare treat her so; her heart turned to ice at the possibility of who else it might be.

She stood stiff as a corpse, locked in the tight embrace of strong arms, her eyes round and searching the darkness for any way to free herself. If only Matty had been truthful and told her where he was to be off to, but if these were pirates, maybe he'd been captured, too.

Closing her eyes, Christine braced herself for abuse, but she was not knocked to the ground. Instead, a heavy canvas bag snapped over her head, and she screeched again, fearful she would suffocate. Tripping over her own feet and her captor's boots, she stumbled to the ground but was scooped up before she fell flat. The world was black now, and she was blind. The bag reeked of fermented grain, and she gasped for air. Not even the roguish Captain Butler would treat her this way.

The rough bag scraped her nose and cheeks as Christine sucked in another breath. They would suffocate her before they could murder her. She'd be dead before they could ravage her in the marsh.

Shaking with terror, she broke into wild kicks and punches against her captor until he dumped her to the ground. She tried to crawl away, but he pinned her hands to her sides and tied her down, then hissed at her to be quiet and with one easy scoop, threw her over his shoulder and made her dizzy until she lost her bearings.

Struggling to breathe, she was little aware of being tossed into the bottom of a wet, foul-smelling boat. Muffled voices paddled it away into the river bottoms where she suspected they would leave her body to rot.

Instead, an excruciating length of time later and with no warning, she was shaken out of her stupor and bounced about in the air until someone plopped her onto a hard, unforgiving surface. Her bottom smacked painfully into hard planks, and she smelled tar and oakum. Jerked to consciousness, she saw a dim light through her blindfold and almost fainted with relief when it was pulled from her head.

Finally, cool blessed air, and she could breathe. She gasped for air and looked down. Her arms were still tied to her sides, and her hems were coated with mud and seawater.

"You're more trouble than you're worth," came a growl from behind, and she twisted around to see the face of Alligator George before he executed her. A heavy fist caught her head by the hair and forced it forward. She was in a cabin. In front of her was a narrow cot; beside it a small table and oil lamp.

She swallowed in fear. Her family's smuggling problems would be nothing compared to being captured by pirates. They'd never see her again.

The man behind her grunted. "You could have been shot—should have been—but then I'd have had to deal with questions, and I have no time for them."

The voice sounded familiar. Christine sniffed. Was she mistaken?

"Fortunately for you, I am fond of your brother."

"Captain Butler?" She ducked out from under his heavy hand and looked over her shoulder again. Captain Butler towered over her. His hands were on his hips, and he sported muddy black boots and breeches. A white shirt lay open at the neck, with no waistcoat and no cravat, and his hair was mussed—windblown and untidy. A sheen of sweat shined across his forehead.

"Lawks," she gasped. Her mouth gaped, and she took a deep, raspy breath to refill her lungs. "You—you—"

He didn't smile or chuckle but thumped past her and collapsed onto the cot. She spun around and found him staring like a cat about to spring. With knees splayed, he leaned forward and clasped his hands. She shrank back from his fists, just inches from her nose. His dark brows were low and furrowed over his glimmering, glaring eyes. His mouth had fallen into its grim line.

Christine stared back in amazement until she found her tongue. "How dare you treat me so! Kidnapping is worse than smuggling. You're nothing but a common criminal!"

He listened to her rebukes without a word. Christine huffed. "I thought you were a pirate."

With no expression, he blurted, "I am a pirate, Miss Fryer. Congratulations. You've been kidnapped by Alligator George."

Christine felt her mouth slack open, and the truth became clear in her mind. She let her lips curl in revulsion. The horror. It was all she could do not to collapse. "You. You're Alligator George." She felt a sudden panic for her brother. "What have you done with Matty?"

"Nothing," Captain Butler snapped, "and don't be hysterical. Your brother is not a pirate and neither am I."

"But you just said—"

He dropped his hands and reared back. "I am not a pirate," he insisted in a loud, sharp tone. "It's a farce, a story I found convenient to perpetuate. None of us are. True, we avoid port with some of our shipments, but it's nothing more than a little smuggling as you surmised."

Christine gazed into his crystal eyes and searched for truth and honor. He looked at the beams overhead as if gathering his patience. "You were right the first time. Alligator George is our disguise."

"But my brother—"

"Is on his way back to Savannah. His lumber yard anyway."

Christine struggled to her feet. "Untie me at once," she ordered. She wobbled in her riding boots.

"No. Sit down, or I'll tie you to a chair."

She gaped in surprise. Captain Butler unfolded to his full stature as he stood up. The top of his head nearly reached the boards over his head.

"Where am I?"

"You're aboard the *Siren*," he said, arching a brow.

"You mean the *Dragon*," she spat. "You brought me aboard a pirate ship."

"The *Dragon* is not real. It's just a convenient legend. Now hush and let me think."

Christine sank to her knees again, but she was unable to tame her tongue. Perhaps it was Papa's influence. Maybe she was more like him than she thought. "You can't keep me tied up like this. I'll—"

"You'll what?"

Captain Butler began to pace. It was a small cabin, and he seemed to fill it up with each stride.

Christine settled into a crouch on the boards beneath her. "How dare you," she repeated in a mumbling voice. Her mind spun. Was he really Alligator George? It explained everything, but if it were true, what did that mean for her? A slender arrow of fear tore through her thumping heart.

"You've ruined everything, Christine," Captain Butler said, dropping her title. He clapped his hands and continued his striding back and forth across the room. "This was my last trip—my last shipment under their noses—and your brother would be out, and so would I."

"Let me go." Christine refused to listen to his excuses. "I need to find Matty."

"I told you. He's fine and on his way home."

"No!" Christine shouted, not caring who heard. "Papa and Mr. Hawthorne looked at his accounts and saw they don't add up."

Captain Butler stopped his marching and stared at her.

"They know his income exceeds what's on the ledgers. Papa is going to question him as soon as he returns. They've shown the numbers to Gabble's bookkeeper. I have to find him and warn him."

The captain's face crumpled into frustration. He pounded his fist into an open hand. "Blast your father and his prying! He's been sniffing around every time I'm in port asking questions."

Christine nodded. "Probably. He and Mr. Hawthorne made an investment in Matty's business and want to see it succeed. They believe you ship for him—legally."

Butler put his hands on his hips and let out a slow breath. "I do carry some loads above the boards." As if distracted, he raised a brow at her. "Does he call often, Hawthorne?"

Christine scowled at him. "What does it matter? Untie me. I have to get home before I'm discovered missing."

"No."

"What?"

He studied her for a moment, and Christine wiggled her shoulders and twisted in her bindings to get his attention. "You can't keep me bound like this. I'll have a rash. Let me go!"

"I can't," he said slowly, shaking his head. He marched across the room and swung open the door.

"Captain Butler!"

"Keep quiet, Miss Fryer," he called on his way out. "I must see to Mathew, so I'll have to deal with you later." He left her in a hot, dripping pile in the middle of the floor.

CHAPTER SEVEN

Nathan scribbled a hasty message to Mathew, sealed it, then called for Isaac. The old sailor was lurking nearby, probably anxious to learn what they would do with the troublesome girl in the cabin. Nathan handed him the warning note and rested his hand on the trusted man's shoulder to express his regrets.

"I'm sorry," he said in the quiet. They stood along the bulwark with the last skiff waiting below. The barrels of rice and lumber were aboard, but now because of Miss Fryer, there would be one last delay.

"I can be back before sunrise," insisted Isaac. He looked with concern at the rest of the crew preparing to tow the *Siren* out to sea.

Nathan shook his head. "It's impossible. We must get out before we're spotted loitering around the waterway. We left port at dawn so people would wonder why the *Siren* is still about."

Isaac made a grumbling noise in his throat.

"We must warn him," Nathan insisted. "Deliver the message to Fryer and return to Clearwater. We'll pick you up on our return and carry you back into port since you're on the books this time."

"What about the girl?" Isaac's voice came out a growl.

"Thank you for not shooting her." Nathan squeezed his shoulder. He grunted. "I can think of nothing to do but carry her with me to the Indies."

"I could get her back to shore."

"That was my first thought, but look." Nathan nodded toward the eastern sky. "She will never make it home before daylight. They are going to know she's missing, and it would be worse if someone spied her with you."

Nathan rubbed his forehead, the small thudding of a headache beginning to squeeze under the surface. "I can think of nothing else to do with her. I'll set her loose after we return to port and invent a story. Maybe we can say we rescued her."

"From Alligator George?" Isaac chuckled over his palpable disappointment at missing their last run.

Nathan dipped his chin in agreement. "Something like that. For now, return to the house and stay out of sight. We should be back in a matter of weeks if luck holds out. Have the servants spread the story—a rumor—that Alligator George kidnapped a girl out walking in the marsh. At least her father will know it was her."

Isaac nodded, added one last mumble of annoyance over being cut off from a voyage to the Indies then leaped into the netting hanging over the side. Nathan watched his little skiff row away into the murk then ordered the boats adrift of the bow to begin their stroking to tow the *Siren* back downriver toward the open sea.

RHYTHMIC CREAKING AND swaying brought Christine into a slow and confused state of wakefulness. She realized she was not in a dream even before her eyes opened. Hearing the voices of sailors on deck, she knew she was aboard a ship—Captain Butler's smuggling ship, whatever he pretended to call it.

With great, exhausting effort, she forced her eyelids to open and found herself staring sideways at the oakum between the ship's planking. The tar's odor was a distant smell in her memory; she had not been on many boats in her life, but she'd grown up around them. With a groan, she sat up and looked at her hands.

The ropes were gone. So were her muddy boots. She was sitting on the cot. As her sleepy fog cleared, Christine realized someone had untied her and put her to bed, although she was still dressed. With a start, she saw her gown draped over the back of the chair and the hastily unpinned stomacher lying on the small table beside her. She lifted the thin coverlet spread over her and looked down. She was in her shift, and her stained stockings were pulled up to her knees.

"Ugh," she moaned, thirsty and hot. She crawled out and peered into a pitcher of water on the small table. A chamber pot was pushed under the cot.

Washing her face and the rest of her body, Christine stole quick peeks over her shoulder should someone come in. She shook out her gown and re-dressed then slipped on her riding boots. Next, she combed her hair with her fingers. With few pins, there was nothing to do but braid it in a single chain and let it hang down her back. Christine prayed the captain was on deck, and with a final breath of determination, pushed open the door and marched out into the day's early light.

At once, she found herself tottering back and forth as she dashed the few steps to the nearest mast. The earth and sky moved past the ship, and men hovered overhead in the lines. As unfurled sails filled with wind pushed the ship forward, her stomach lurched. "Oh no," she cried to none of the crew around her. "We're moving!"

They ignored her. Christine put her hand on the mast to steady herself. All around her the ship bustled with activity. The horizon glowed orange with just a hint of morning sun peeking over it. A whipping, salty breeze snapped the canvas, and the sound of the waves rushing past the ship's hull made a splashing hum.

"You're awake, I see."

Christine turned to face Captain Butler. "Must you always sneak up on me, and why are we moving? Where are we going? Wait," she cried. She watched the outer banks drift by. "We're sailing south."

Captain Butler nodded once in agreement. He wore the same clothes as the night before, but he'd tidied up and looked more in control of himself.

Christine pondered what this meant as she studied him. "You're not taking me home."

"I'm not." His face looked drawn and serious. There was no flirting or even pretending that he was a gentleman now.

She squared her shoulders. "Captain Butler, you must take me back to Savannah." Her mind spun. "Matty!"

"Calm yourself. I've taken care of your brother. He will be warned. As far as his accounts, I can't help you there, but he should have been more careful." Captain Butler sounded like a stern parent.

"What about me?" demanded Christine. "I need to get home."

He put his hands on his hips and shrugged like she didn't matter at all. "It's too late for that, Miss Fryer. You should have stayed in your bed."

Christine looked around in amazement. "You're not taking me with you to the Caribbean? On wild and illegal business? I think not. Drop me off at Darian, and I shall fend for myself."

"I considered throwing you overboard once we were out to sea, but with my luck, you'd turn into a mermaid and follow us back." Captain Butler motioned toward the bow. "Unfortunately, Miss Fryer, you're joining us on our voyage to the Leewards, and your father will not be informed."

"You can't do this." Christine heard her own voice raise to a hysterical pitch, but she didn't care. "My papa will think I ran away. He may think I'm dead."

The man before her took a threatening step closer. "You'll wish you were dead once they get the news." He reached out for her hand, but she stepped back into the mast behind her.

"What news?" she answered in a low, angry tone. She wanted to slap the careless look right off his hard, chiseled face.

"I'm sorry to tell you," continued Captain Butler in his flat tone, "that you have been 'kidnapped' by Alligator George after all."

Silence fell over the ship as she struggled to understand. She realized the entire crew was listening and enjoying her tantrum. She grit her teeth and said in a hard voice, "You can't spread a rumor like that. You said he's a farce, a legend. You're not really a pirate—so let me go." She shuddered with shame that she was pouting so.

"We've no other choice," said Captain Butler, but this time he sounded apologetic.

"You do have a choice. Give me a boat, and I'll row back to Savannah myself."

The captain laughed. It was a loud, amused sound that came from his stomach and echoed off the canvas sails. "I'm sorry Miss Fryer, but you're my prisoner now." He didn't sound sorry.

Christine stared at him in disbelief. Would he really drag her off to sea and ruin her reputation? "Don't do this," she pleaded, her voice breathless with dread.

"I have no choice." Captain Butler pointed toward the cabin. "Go back to your little hiding-hole and stay put. I'll have someone bring you food and ale."

Christine didn't move. No matter how handsome he was, no matter how clever or rich or mysterious he appeared to be, she could not sail to the Indies with a smuggler—or pirate. Her stomach rolled over, and she realized she was nauseated to the point of vomiting.

"Go," said Captain Butler, ordering her like one of his men, "or I'll throw you over my shoulder and take you back myself." His mouth twitched like he was fighting back a grin, and she guessed he'd enjoy it very much.

Christine's mind swirled with more arguments, but she didn't want to be treated like a sack of oats again. He made a move toward her, and she dashed past him. "I'm going," she retorted, furious and afraid and wondering what would become of her. "Don't you touch me," she warned. "Don't you ever touch me again." She didn't want him to know that a part of her liked when they'd danced, but kidnapping her had been terrifying. It was a confusing, muddled mess. She stormed back to her room.

WITH CHRISTINE FRYER stowed away in his sleeping quarters, Nathan sat on the other side of the thin bulkhead at his table. It served as a desk and as a dining table. He flipped through charts and tried to focus. Mr. Walker marched in and shut the door behind him, closing off a most welcome breeze.

"Have we left the coast behind?" Nathan didn't look up.

Mr. Walker pulled out a narrow chair across from the table and dropped into it. "There's no land in sight, just the horizon ahead."

"I thought so," said Nathan. "How does the weather glass look?"

"It looks well enough. I don't expect rain tonight."

"Could be rougher," murmured Nathan to himself.

"We'll sail directly to the cove?" asked the officer, and Nathan nodded.

"I have no plans to stop in St. John this time 'round. It'd be best to vary our routine at this point in the game."

Mr. Walker nodded but looked pensive. "What about the woman? The merchant's daughter?"

Nathan leaned back in his chair. "I'll take care of it. She won't be a problem."

"The crew's concerned. We've sailed without trouble nearly a half-dozen years indulging in our... salutary neglect."

"Yes, well," agreed Nathan, "the rules have changed under the Constitution, and they are enforcing them." He shrugged.

"Our country has tariffs now, and we must obey them—after this last run."

Walker gave a slight nod. "I've yet to receive pay for the last six months of the war." He lifted a shoulder in a careless motion. "I figure we're even now—Washington and me."

"It's just been half-shipments from the Indies," agreed Nathan, "we're not the worst kind to bypass the ports, but it's time for a fresh start. An honest one. No one can compensate me for the British seizing my city and driving my father to hang himself, so I've gone and done it myself. After this, our accounts are settled, like you said."

Walker let out a heavy breath. "And if the girl tattles?"

"Like I told you," Nathan said leaning forward, "if she breathes a word her brother will be exposed, and her family ruined." He snorted. "If Hawthorne knew her involvement, he'd tell Fryer to stay out of our business."

Nathan pushed over a chart, and Walker gave him his advice for their route around the Virgin Islands and through the Leewards. At the turn of the glass, the bell rang, and the crew exchanged their positions from above deck to below. Nathan climbed down to the galley and collected a plate of cheese and old biscuit for his prisoner. Returning to the cabin, he knocked on his own private door and waited for her to reply. "Miss Fryer?"

There was a rustling behind the door before she opened it slowly. Miss Fryer didn't bother to take the platter. Her face looked milky white, and bruise-colored smudges made crescent shapes under her eyes. Nathan was sure if he stepped back and examined her better she'd have a greenish cast about her; he knew the look of a landlubber's first days at sea.

She opened her mouth and took a gaspy breath. "No," she whispered.

"You're ill?"

"I'm..." She licked her lips and managed to say, "I feel unwell. The motion of the ship and the..." She swallowed, and he took a step back in case she retched over his boots.

"I'm sorry. Would some bread help?"

She shook her head, stepped away, and wilted onto the cot. The ship danced over a wave and down its backside, and Nathan adjusted his stance to move as one with the motion.

He glanced at the plate in his hand. "I'm sorry you're sick." He was. He felt miserable for her. Seasickness was a horrible thing, and it could go on for days. If she wasn't already furious with him for kidnapping her, she would certainly hate him now.

"I'll just set this here," he told her, not knowing what more to do. For a woman who walked with confidence and carried a healthy, robust glow in her cheeks, she looked diminutive and ghostly now.

When she didn't respond, Nathan moved over to the stumpy table beside the cot and set down the food. He studied her long hair. It was let down and combed out, a thick coil of coffee-dark auburn waves that looked as soft as satin. He stepped back, surprised at himself. Yes, he'd always noticed her rose-bud mouth because of the way it set off her dusted complexion, but he'd never put much thought into the dark hair she wore pinned up around her face—other than to admire the streaks of light in it that shimmered like late sunset.

"Captain?" someone called.

Nathan jumped at the bosun's voice and hurried out so as not to disturb the wretched girl further. This was his fault, dragging her along. Perhaps he should have set her loose in the marsh with a good swap on her horse's hindquarters, but she would have been discovered and had to answer for herself, even if she did not betray his ship. Nathan's chest felt as heavy as marsh mud when he closed the door behind him.

CHRISTINE'S LIFE BECAME a living nightmare. One moment, she'd been walking across the square admiring trees and the summer blooms on the flowers, and the next she'd been snatched from the dark marsh and thrown into a room that moved up and down and side to side until she thought she would vomit up her toes. It seemed the cruel torture would never end.

After what she could only surmise was the fifth day aboard the *Siren*, Christine forced down another cup of tea at Captain Butler's insistence and decided she felt well enough to wash and redress. He'd loaned her a tunic to do as a shift and ordered her clothing washed. She was not even ashamed that the crew had seen her petticoat and underthings because they were so clean and smelled so wonderful it didn't matter enough.

When she heard the noonday bell clatter, she took another nibble of dried ginger and tiptoed out of the sleeping quarters of the captain's cabin. The forward room of his personal space was sparsely furnished with an oblong table framed by chairs and a sideboard covered with more nautical instruments and books than dishes. A cutlass hung suspended over the door, but as far as any other weapons, she could only suppose they were locked up in an armory somewhere below. With a deep breath, Christine exited the cabin and took a few wobbly steps down the long, narrow deck.

The crew on deck ignored her, or at least they pretended to. She weaved her way through stacked supplies and around stiff rigging until she found a spot along the rail where she would be out of the way. Looking up at the clear sky decorated with only the occasional puff of glowing white cloud, she noted the *Siren* had two masts and a long bowsprit. There was a rather rickety crow's nest on the foremast, and at the stern of the ship sat a great wheel to draw in the anchor. A few men looked superior to the others in their clean white tunics and dark cocked hats.

Captain Butler had his back to her but turned the instant she began to consider the shape of his lean waist and the inversion of his wide shoulders which carried his weight. His dark hair ruffled in the brisk wind snapping over the deck, and his eyes glowed from the distance. She jerked her head back to the horizon's view and put both hands on the rail to concentrate on the rise and fall of the vessel over the swells.

Boots echoed on the boards beneath Christine's feet, and she sensed someone behind her. She dared another look.

"Miss Fryer," said the bosun with a slight bow. She recognized him as a man of some rank. His voice was often shouting at others or making belligerent noises.

Christine stiffened her shoulders. "I won't go back to my room," she said, forcing her tone to sound stubborn and brave.

He fiddled with a cap that he'd been pleasant enough to remove upon addressing her then cleared his throat.

"I need some air and a view other than from a crack in the boards."

"We don't want yeh to be bumped or tripped over," he said in stern reply.

Christine could tell he was trying to be patient, but she kept her back to him. "I'll stay out of the way," she insisted. She pretended not to see him anymore and to think about something else.

"Miss Fryer."

Christine recognized the new voice. It sent a rush of little chills down her back. She kept her gaze trained on the distant sky.

"I am feeling a little better, thank you."

Captain Butler chuckled. "I was going to ask, but I'm happy to see you up and looking less green this morning."

The reminder that he'd seen her in her pitiful state and knew she'd been tossing up her stomach for days made Christine's cheeks hot. She glanced over her shoulder. Captain Butler was a different kind of handsome at sea, she decided. Not trussed up in stiff cravats or scraping and bowing to anyone of importance. She wondered which was his true nature and which was the disguise.

"I do feel less green."

He stepped up beside her and leaned over the rail but not without glancing at her first. "If you've held down your breakfast that's progress. Shall I give you a tour? Come, let us stretch our legs a bit. I've been at the con since sunrise, and I'm restless."

He held out an arm, and she glanced into his face before she took it. He was looking at her the way a mother watched a child with concern, and she dropped her searching gaze before he saw the confusion she felt.

Captain Butler was a scoundrel with a salty, cold heart. He circumvented the ports to avoid tariffs and other laws and was a dreadful influence on her brother. Why was he being kind now?

He held out a hand, and she grudgingly took it. Arm in arm, he led her on a slow stroll around the ship, dodging the ratlines and stopping occasionally to point out a new block and tackle or replaced planking.

"I have a few associates at our destination," he said as they ambled along. "If there is time and the situation is appropriate, I know of a place you may lodge for a few days. The innkeeper's wife will watch over you and provide you with a companion should you like to explore the island."

"Explore?" Christine almost laughed. She'd never been to the Indies. It was a whimsical notion in her mind, and a dangerous one, too.

"It's not all that gruesome," Captain Butler said with a grin. "The islands are a beautiful scene with exotic trees and fruit you won't believe. And the weather is fair most days and the breezes heavenly. Not to mention, you won't find more beautiful waters than on the shores of the Indies."

"I guess that's why the pirates like it so."

He chuckled at her retort. "I suppose so, once upon a time. There is little to fear for that lot with the man-o-wars and privateers keeping our waters in check."

"Then how do you get about?" She eyed him curiously. A part of her wanted to hear his excuses. They'd crossed to the other rail, the larboard side, and he guided her into a corner between piles of rolled canvas. "I get about just fine because I'm an American and a merchant ship."

Christine pursed her lips but resisted the urge to cross her arms. She looked up with a steady stare. "But you're not a merchant."

He smiled a little bit then let it drop off with a tilt of his head. "I am completely legitimate, I assure you. I only carry a few unchecked goods that circumvent the officials before I make port."

"As you do in Savannah," accused Christine.

He narrowed his eyes. "You are certainly inclined to disapprove of any form of additional income outside of inheritances."

"I believe in keeping the law," she replied.

"And your father was a patriot?" He chuckled. "Not a loyalist? Are you sure?"

She huffed. "Certainly not. My brother, James, died at their hands. Papa sent me away to his second cousin who lived south of us near Darien. I spent years of my childhood hiding from British sails and Indians in a very small home believing the world was over."

"That must have been most unpleasant."

"Yes, especially since our mother died before the first shots were fired. Matty and I thought we would be orphaned, and so before I was sent away we made a pact to watch out for one another if we survived." Remembering Mathew's solemn words and his penknife that had pricked her finger when she was a little girl, Christine held it up proudly. "A blood pact," she added.

"Impressive." Captain Butler's tone rang with teasing, and she dropped her arm from his. "That's why I must look out for him, you see. He has no mother or no elder brother to guide him on his way."

"So little Christine is his conscience?"

"A guide," she snapped back. Clearly, the man was not impressed with her devotion to Matty, and here he did not appear to have any family at all.

He seemed to sense her affront and said, "I admire your brother and that he has someone so devoted to his welfare. I'm sure he'll be the better for it. I know he adores you, for he speaks of you with the highest regard."

The pleasing compliment lifted Christine's mood. "I don't know what he shall do when I'm married off and put away," she blurted. A knot of apprehension found its way up to her throat. She blinked away threatening tears and stared at the light smudge of clouds just over the horizon. The sun was halfway up to the heavens, and it'd grown much warmer, but the sea breeze washing over the *Siren* made it tolerable.

"Well," said Captain Butler after a pause, "I wish you luck with that and... Hawthorne is it?" He was teasing her again. Christine sniffed, sneaked a glance at him, and found him grinning.

"Absolutely not," she insisted. Mr. Hawthorne and Papa seemed far away, like specters in an old dream. "I have no intention of marrying Mr. Hawthorne," she said, pleased at the confidence in her tone. She'd never said it out loud. She'd been afraid to, avoiding it, but now she was certain she had made up her mind.

"I'm sure he'll be quite disappointed."

"Yes," she agreed, her bravado wilting, "and so will Papa." Christine breathed hard and looked up. "He will be angry, my papa, and I will find living under our roof as unpleasant as ever." She wondered if Dolly's family would take her in.

"Perhaps Mr. Hawthorne will not be so keen as to marry a woman who's been kidnapped by pirates." Captain Butler chuckled. Then in a turn, he said in a sincere voice, "I apologize for your present situation. As I explained once you were aboard, I had no other choice."

She grimaced. "I only went out to the marsh to find Matty. I'm trying to protect my family and now, to be honest, you've made it worse."

Rather than disagree as to who was at fault, Captain Butler said in a tight voice, "I'm sure we can come up with some sort of story."

"For a month? A season? How long do you intend to keep me away?"

The captain's pleasant countenance faded. "For as little time as possible, I assure you." He sounded hard and cordial again. "And you will keep this secret, Miss Fryer, for all of our sakes."

Once again, he was giving her orders. He was not asking, he was telling—forcing her as she had been forced all her life. Christine clasped her hands on the rail and ignored him, but he was not finished.

"If you are feeling better, perhaps I should put you to work."

She raised her brows in surprise. "I thought I was a guest, Captain Butler. Now, what will you have me do? Scrub the deck? Wash the coppers?"

He looked at her with such disappointment that it pricked her heart. She hadn't meant to suggest she was lazy.

"You can stitch, I presume," he said in a cool tone. "We have mounds of mending always to be done. If you're going to keep my bed and eat our stores, the least you can do is work a needle and thread."

Christine sniffed. She wanted to refuse and rebel, but it was not more than she was willing to do, and she did not mean to pace his cabin for weeks on end with no activity. "Very well," she relented.

"I thank you then." He seemed pleased at her submission, and it irritated her.

"It's the least I can do," she mumbled, "although I'm the one who was kidnapped." With a curt curtsy, she stumbled back toward the confines of her room.

"You may join me for dinner," he called at her back, and even though it carried on the wind, she didn't turn around. Ordering her where to eat he could not do.

CHAPTER EIGHT

After a few days of allowing his guest to pout with the sewing in his cabin in the heat of the afternoon, and promenading with her on deck in the evenings, Nathan felt relieved when land was sighted. They had drifted past the British's Virgin islands, later hailed a friendly Spanish merchant ship with no trouble, and made it safely to within reach of the southern leeward islands. He would sail about Martinique, land in a cove near St. William known as *la Chaîne Solide*, and deliver his rice, honey, and lumber to his buyer. A full load back with sugar and molasses would finish the tour.

Almost satisfied and near-comfortable with their safety, he left the con with a rumbling stomach and his chest burning over the mild indignation he felt for Miss Fryer—or Miss Christine—as he had taken upon himself to think of her. She'd refused to join him for dinner after each invitation since they'd left the inlet, and she was no longer ill. He rapped on her partition.

"Yes?"

Nathan took that as permission to enter and pushed open the door. Christine sat near the small porthole on a short stool. She was hunched over a pile of cloth, and he saw it was a pair of his buckskin breeches. Split aside at the knee, he'd tossed them aside for future repair, and she'd picked it up from the mending pile and set to work fixing the seam. She looked up and a lock of her shining hair fell across her forehead.

"Yes?" she repeated.

He stopped short, surprised at the blow to his chest the image gave him. She looked like a sprite who'd stowed away in his cabin.

"I, uh, Miss Christine," he said with a nod. "Mr. Walker appreciates you replacing the button on his cuff."

She sat up and arched her back like it pained her. "I'm only following orders," she said with impertinence then broke into a grin. "Really, I don't mind it, and I appreciate him loaning me his copy of *Common Sense* although it is a bit dry and tiresome reading for me."

Nathan walked in and stood across from her. "Paine has written a new one, you know. *Rights of Man*."

"Yes, I know. Papa has it." She slanted her head. He forgot she was so quick and intelligent, an admirable quality that made her more handsome.

"Let me assure you," she teased, "I have no intention of encouraging an uprising on your decks."

"Let's hope not," he chuckled. "Forgive me. I thank you for your help with the mending, but I must apologize for not inviting you to dine this night."

She raised a brow in ridicule. "I have not accepted any of your invitations to dine. The last thing you need, I suspect, is a lady at your table with the wardroom when you already have to deal with me amidship."

He couldn't disagree with her, but he did enjoy her company, and the wardroom could well control their tongues for a time with a woman in their midst. "Well," he said, blinking away the surprise at her good humor, "I've come to inform you we have our landing within sight and will be slinking into *la Chaîne Solide* at dark. We'll drop anchor soon and row into the cove."

The news perked her interest. "At last?" She stood up in a rush and put her forehead to the porthole.

"You're looking the wrong way," he chuckled, and she pulled back. "I must come out then. I've watched the distant islands pass by and could make out nothing. Will you show it to me?"

He grinned and held out an arm, and she tossed the breeches onto the neatly made cot and joined him.

On deck, he walked her past the capstan and pointed out the distant smudge of the northwest cap of Martinique. He identified sails in the distance as other merchants and a small untroubled naval sloop carrying mail, and she clapped with excitement.

"I was beginning to feel like I'd never see God's green earth again."

He chuckled. "It gets that way."

"And you'll let me off? On the morrow?"

He glanced at her, encouraged by her excitement, but sad to disappoint her. "I'm sorry to tell you, that you must stay put until we unload on the cay and then we will make a short trip to the harbor of the small island of St. William. It would be best for you to stay in the cabin until then."

Instead of getting angry, Christine sighed. "I suppose I can survive one more day."

"Good girl," he said, letting the formalities between them slip. "I mean, lovely," he stuttered. She gave him a flitting look then returned to the view. "And you are rowing out to a cove?" She hesitated. "Is it safe?"

He ducked his head but could not bring himself to nod all of the way. "It's... Well, we will drop anchor at sunset and wait until dark. Then a party will tow out the goods." He motioned aft with his chin. "Mr. Walker will have the ship. You could be in no safer company."

Christine looked at Nathan in surprise, and narrow pink rays of sunshine lit up her face. "Am I in danger?"

"No, of course not." He forced a smile. It was better for her not to know what a French Indies prison would be like if they were caught.

"What if the ship is recognized?"

"Most men would run."

She crinkled her forehead. "From the *Siren*?"

"From the *Dragon*. We are now in disguise."

"Oh. My goodness. The ship of Alligator George?" She cleared her throat and looked away like she was deciding whether or not to believe him. "Captain Butler," she said in a serious voice, "what happens if you and the men are caught? Alligator George is quite a legend, isn't he?"

"We won't be," said Nathan, wishing she would not curse them so. He already had a woman on board.

Christine gazed at the distant shadow of Martinique. "Do they hang smugglers in the Caribbean, Captain Butler," she asked.

"Some of them," Nathan admitted.

He tried to force down the thudding of his now anxious heart. Every delivery, even under cover of night, was a risk, but he'd never let himself think beyond excusing himself with ignorance of other empires' laws, his nationality, or a bribe if that would do.

He knew if anyone searched his vessel they'd find evidence she was more than a rumored little pirate ship—she was an American merchantman, the *Siren*, in disguise.

WITH NIGHTFALL CAME the longest night of Christine's life, and she admitted she'd felt some excitement for visiting the West Indies. Her fear and fury of being snatched from the marsh had slowly turned into reluctant acceptance as the days had passed. The murmur of water beneath the hull, and the pleasant wind and fresh air had quieted her concerns. She'd pushed the horror of what Papa and the rest of Savannah would think to the furthest corners of her mind. In a vivid sapphire sea and under skies as blue as cornflowers, she'd inadvertently embraced her situation—and her captor. Their daily walks had become frank and intimate and something to look forward to.

She tossed over on the lumpish cot in the darkness. The hot air stood still, even as the ship fluttered over the calm surface of the water, turning in aimless circles on a single anchor in the night. The crew had become quieter at sunset, as if even a whisper might float all the way to Basseterre. The lanterns were doused and smoke was not allowed.

There was hardly a moon to be seen, and the stars looked distant and dull. Frustrated with the dread hanging in the air, Christine crawled out of her cot and stood at the porthole staring into the darkness. Her pulse sounded heavy and loud in her ears. Her stomach twisted with apprehension.

Captain Butler had touched her elbow as if to comfort her as he explained what would happen tonight. It'd been a natural, innocent gesture, but it had sent a surging ripple of heat up her arm and into her chest where it stayed tingling for a time. It bothered her, the strange wanting, and she instructed herself to ignore it.

She'd watched them lower the anchor as violet rays of light glimmered from the horizon in the distance. Once the cargo was sent overboard into the longboats below, she slipped out of the way so she did not stand there like a girl desperate for a last goodbye.

What more could he say? This was his business, and she had interfered with it. There was no reason to complain and there was nothing she could do now that would change his stubborn mind.

When she noticed the ship's sails had been changed out and that a wooden plaque hung over the *Siren's* hand-painted name on the stern, she realized she was now on a pirate ship. They lowered their country's red and white striped flag with its fifteen stars, and Christine forced herself to return to the cabin and shut the door. If they flew a jolly roger, she did not want to see it.

She pressed her forehead against the porthole and looked out into the night. She mumbled a prayer that Captain Butler would be safe on his last expedition—and forgiven. Though she didn't understand all of the reasons he rationalized his evasion of import charges, she felt hopeful that as a true American, he would pay his share now and still make a profit.

Mathew had confided to her after the meeting in his room, that Clearwater had been rebuilt and was filled with all kinds of fine rugs and furnishings. Since it was so far away from the cobblestones of Savannah, Christine knew she would like to see this house and wondered if the captain was lonely there with the ghosts of his father and wives. Perhaps that was why he wandered around in the marsh.

A loud, deep boom echoed overhead, and Christine jumped. *Captain Butler! Nathan!* Fear racing through her veins, she dashed to the door and rested her ear against it. Cannons. Had he been shot? She thought she heard the faint tones of the officers still aboard, but no one reacted to the sound and nothing changed.

After a few moments, she returned to the porthole and waited, and minutes later distant rumblings across the sky made her realize it hadn't been cannons she'd heard. The ship began to bounce up and down on its line. Lightning lit up the darkness, and Christine retreated to the cot to stay dry, but she could not sleep. She jerked with fear as a summer thunderstorm blew over the night, and worried over the fate of her brother's trusted confidant and her wary, tentative friend.

She awoke with a start. Golden sunbeams danced through the porthole, and the ship rocked less violently than before. Christine scrambled off of the cot, wavering to catch her balance. She had not undressed should they be caught by any Frenchmen monitoring their cays, so she patted down her hair, rearranged her petticoats, and hurried out onto deck.

The *Siren* was the *Siren* once more. Christine looked up and saw the American red and white flag flying as they came around a most breathtaking scene. A green leafy tangle of feathery trees floated past. They lined a strip of white sandy shore that looked magical against the lightest and bluest water she'd ever seen.

She gasped in surprise and rushed over to the rail to look down. As azure as a gemstone, the glowing water slid over the side of the ship making a foamy, fairy-blue wake behind them. The shallows stroked the distant shore like a calm whisper, and small mountains in the distance, hills really, beckoned her to come explore.

Someone called from the crow's nest, and Christine followed the pointing finger. In the distance, the enormous island seemed to draw back, and she could make out a jumble of tall masts and galley windows from a great many ships moored all together in a deep water harbor. They were coming into St. William's port!

She looked and saw Captain Butler at the bow with a man holding a sounding line, and her heart warmed with relief. He was safe. They all were. She must have slept through his quiet return. The crew had safely delivered their illegal cargo and returned to sail the rest of the way into this exotic port. Butler would pay some tariffs now, shake hands with his French contacts, and all would be well. For now. They would not return to Savannah until he resupplied, she guessed, loaded with the sugar, molasses, and the rum that all of the young American states craved.

She nibbled her lip and studied Captain Butler. Nathan, Matty called him. She'd thought of him as Nathan last night.

He seemed tired but content, his jaw in need of a shave and his hair loose, but she could forgive him since he had not gotten himself caught last night. At the rail, she drank in the exotic scenery around her until they came into the harbor slinking past the other boats.

Christine blinked in the sunshine then remembered her state of dress and rushed back into the cabin to change. It seemed like hours before the steward came to fetch her.

The inn, where Nathan had promised to deposit her, sat above a knoll on an uphill walk from the colorful harbor. The lodging was quaint but clean with whitewashed coral and timber beams. A swinging board over the front door proclaimed it to be *The Pearled Toby.*

"I think you'll be satisfied here," he declared, and she smiled her appreciation. There was a parlor downstairs for visiting and tea, another room for guests to dine, and a narrow staircase that led up to a few small rooms with low ceilings.

For some reason, Christine had assumed he would take a room at a lodging elsewhere or stay aboard his ship, but Captain Butler took the room across the hall from her. A part of her mind almost shuddered at the impropriety of being a single woman alone and at sea, but no one seemed to concern themselves with the young lady in the company of a ship's captain and wardroom.

The innkeeper's wife, Madame Bellerose, who wore a high wig and powdered her face, agreed to be her companion. However, after showing Christine to her room and informing her the captain intended to send over a milliner to fit her for a gown and other inexpressibles, the woman disappeared after their introductions. Christine suspected she would not see much of her again.

She walked over to the window overlooking the loud stone street clattering with wagon wheels and street peddlers and drew in a breath of brackish air laced with horse manure. "It's not too different than Savannah," she murmured, and yet, it was. She sank into a sagging bed that felt damp. Outside her window, the island was a beautiful blue and green new world, but she would have to wait for Nathan to show her around as he'd promised.

Despite what she felt should be ladylike reservations, she found the adventure intoxicating and exciting and could hardly wait until the eventide. What would Papa think, she wondered. And why didn't she care?

CHAPTER NINE

With his business affairs in order, Nathan returned to the Pearled Toby and arranged a meal for Christine and himself since they had missed dinner. It was much cooler outside than in, so Madame Bellerose ordered two settings on one of her finest tables in the back courtyard. Nathan was pleased when he saw it had a lovely view of the palm tree groves that edged the lower beaches. There was also a glimpse of the southwestern horizon.

With an inward chiding, he amused himself with the idea of having a solitary dinner with Mathew's sister. He hoped his friend would not mind. He didn't care if Hawthorne did. With the details taken care of, he went up to his room and changed into a fresh shirt and his light waistcoat. A few strokes of pomade tamed his hair, and he assured himself in the looking glass that he'd look ridiculous in a wig.

Across the hall, he knocked on the door belonging to Christine. There was a rustle of fabric, and she opened the door. He inhaled, and it became trapped in his chest. He stared like a ninny. The innkeeper's wife had understandably provided Christine with a lighter, cooler, native gown. Perhaps it was all that she had until the light frock he'd requested arrived.

Christine gave him a sheepish smile. She wore a dazzling white muslin gown without a neckerchief. The long sleeves were a bit short and showed more than her wrists. His eyes traced her décolleté up her slender long neck and then to her rosebud mouth.

Her cheeks colored. "I'm sorry," he said, knowing there was no denying his approving examination. "You caught me off my guard."

She reached for a silk Indian wrap to cover herself. "I feel half-naked, but Madame insists this is suitable." She hesitated.

"We're just supping in the courtyard," he assured her, "and the madame is right. A gown and petticoats are too hot for the Indies on most days, and you've borne enough discomfort. Come outdoors, for the heat of the day is over, and the breeze blowing across the colony is refreshing."

Christine wrapped the shawl around her shoulders and followed him into the hall and down the stairs. He could sense her behind him as her leather-soled slippers matched his footsteps down the steps. When they reached the last one, he offered her his arm, and she took it, allowing him to guide her through the inn and out a side door into a beautiful gated garden dripping with gardenia, bougainvillea, and lemon trees.

He snuck a glance and admired her dark hair. It was plaited under the cotton fichu wrapped around her crown like a turban, and her little earlobes were bare of earbobs. Their nakedness suited her. Her rosy lips were parted in surprise as her eyes widened at the Eden around them.

Nathan chuckled. "I see you are beginning to understand the appeal of the Indies."

She pressed her lips together as if she'd been caught, but her eyes danced with amusement. "I believe I've been enamored since we sailed into your cove."

He smiled at her, and it felt genuine. "We have the courtyard to ourselves." He led her over to the small table draped with woven cloth and a clay pot of bright-colored orchids. Simple china dishes glowed in the low light of a burning lamp.

Christine beamed. "I've never seen such a beautiful scene in all my life, and I've never eaten outside except for a picnic!"

"You'll find your supper tonight to be light but delicious." Nathan chuckled at her zeal. "I never tire of a good curried chicken."

She beamed at him, and he helped her into her seat. As soon as they were settled, she asked about the citrus trees and bougainvillea.

"The vine doesn't grow well in the states," he explained, "but I've seen it in St. Augustine. They say it grows all over Florida."

She *oohed* over the flowers then fell silent as the sinking sun's arms reached the heavens. The sky turned tangerine in a matter of minutes.

He picked up a pitcher of ale while she was captivated and tried not to distract himself with the warm ruby glow reflecting on the apples of her cheeks. "I hope you'll enjoy this place since we are here for a time."

"I already do," she murmured to the sunset. "I feel like I was in Savannah yesterday, and time has somehow stood still, and now I am in paradise."

He smiled at her appreciation of the new surroundings. Perhaps it would help her see the world did not turn only in Savannah. "Then you've forgiven me," he said, and she turned to face him, her mouth puckered in an attempt to fight off a grin.

"Well, I must I suppose, for you only did what had to be done, and I had no choice but to find my brother."

"Let's call a truce. He's safe and informed," Nathan promised her. "I sent a messenger to find him right away. Someone who would not be missed from the crew and is clever enough to not be noticed in town."

Her happy look melted a little. "Oh, I hope so. What trouble that would make." She tightened her smile until it was terse. "I'm sorry that I will be trouble, too, when I return home."

"Don't think of it now," Nathan chided her. "There is nothing to be done until we return, so do not burden yourself."

"Well," she relented, "I'm glad you're here, Captain Butler, and not the dreaded ugly and cruel, Alligator George." She gave a soft giggle, and it made him laugh.

"I'm glad you don't find me ugly, anyway," he teased. He thought he detected a spark of self-reproach in her eyes, and he wondered what it meant. Something pricked his heart and made it heavy.

Dash hope, a surly voice in the back of his head reminded him, *and dash women*. He looked away, pretending to admire the setting sun, and pushed away the dark memories of his father as he welcomed the irritating reminder of Mrs. Blakemore.

Priscilla Blakemore, what a dreadful girl. He sniffed and reached for a handkerchief only to see a buxom servant traipsing down the path to the table cradling a large platter heaped with dinner's re-dressed leftovers. His grumbling stomach took over.

"I'm famished," admitted Christine from across the table, and he nodded in agreement. The servant plied them with rice and beans, dried fish, and cold curried chicken. There were sliced limes and oranges, too.

Smiling, chattering, and full of questions, Christine ate with as great enthusiasm as he did himself, and when they were done, he could not help but offer to walk her down to the sandy shore. They strolled, talking about the flowers in the marsh when compared to the island's floras, until the light sank completely beneath the horizon.

CHAPTER TEN

Despite lying in a stuffy room on a rather uncomfortable bed, Christine slept deeply as the world rocked to and fro just as it had aboard the *Siren*. Nathan had warned her that the world would spin a bit until she found her legs again. She found it queer, but at least it did not make her ill.

The next morning, she made quick work of the breakfast tray sent up from the kitchen. She was impressed with the outdoor kitchen set up behind the inn. It appeared most of the day's food preparations were done in the early hours.

The madame sent up a housemaid to help her dress, and Christine redressed in her clean gown and petticoats and tried not to wish out loud that she could wear the light, flowy chemise dress with the wide ruffle on its hem. Madame also sent up a suitable hat for the sun—an older straw hat with a lovely pink ribbon, and Christine was grateful for the extra protection from the sun it would offer.

She was anxious to depart. The captain had promised to take her on a carriage ride to explore the island before the sun reached its zenith, for later he had a dinner appointment he could not miss with the captain of another merchantman. She'd assured him she preferred to stay inside and read during the heat of the day, and Madame had asked her to tea to continue their discussion on textiles shipped from the East Indies.

Checking the security of her hairpins, Christine picked up the lavender shawl from off the small wardrobe in the simple room and hurried downstairs. At the front window, she stood on her toes and peered outside. Across the street was a milliner's shop; two doors down hunkered a bright green-painted tavern. Horses dragged their loads through the stone-paved streets as children and young women marched back and forth carrying baskets of fruit.

"What do you think of St. William?"

Christine turned at the sound of Nathan's voice. It did not befuddle or frighten her now. Instead, she found it a deep and mellow sound that made her heart stand at attention like a beacon had called her name. She smiled at him, amazed at how fresh and rested he appeared, and how handsome a few hours in the sun made him look.

"I think it's a magical place. I wish I could see all of the isles in the Caribbean."

He chuckled and ran his fingers around the edges of a very light coat—a fetching russet color against his shirt—for once again he had elected not to wear a waistcoat. It made his hair look darker and his eyes as blue as the Caribbean sea.

"I don't suppose you ever tour the Windwards do you?"

"Not if I can help it," he answered. "I prefer to do business as close to home as possible."

"Clearwater?"

"Yes." He watched her like he wanted to know what she thought of it.

A clunking of horse hooves stole her attention, and Nathan motioned out the window at a poor white nag being led around to pull an aged but charming carriage. "Are you ready to explore the island? I think you'll enjoy seeing some of the fine houses up in the hills."

"Yes," smiled Christine, and he led her outside into a fresh breeze that smelled better than the damp streets of home with their human and animal scents on the wind.

He helped her into the carriage, his hand solid and warm as he lifted her. She settled in and patted down her petticoat, pretending that she did not like the sensation of his skin on hers and the warmth of his person close beside her. Her whole body felt tingly with energy and light; a strange, exuberant kind of happiness.

The driver took his seat, gave his whip a crack in the air, and they started down the narrow street back toward the harbor, passing a jumble of shops along the way.

"The apothecary," said Nathan as they passed a small storefront with high windows. It was stocked with glass bell-shaped jars filled with an assortment of things. She noticed a jar of lime peel in the window, and they discussed scurvy and other maladies at sea that dampened her enthusiasm somewhat, especially after his promise there were poisonous trees that could kill a man with just one touch. She made him take an oath that it was true before she would believe him but still, it left her smiling.

They jostled along an uneven road that curved around the edge of the harbor, passing warehouses and offices much like Savannah; but the buildings were not as tall and much lighter. They shined in the sunlight and made the water in the harbor look as blue as the sky.

There was an assortment of ships—French schooners and brigs, a few American vessels, and an army of small fishing boats in various shapes and sizes. There were even canoes and a vast assortment of faces in just as many colors as there were flowers on the island.

"It's a bit utopian, isn't it?" asked Christine as they rode along.

Nathan pointed wordlessly toward a distant plantation and the workers in the fields. They were diminutive from so far away, but very dark. Human chattel.

"Not for everyone," said Nathan in a dark tone. "Not for most people here." Christine bit her lip and felt shame at his reprimand. The driver must have heard, but he said nothing, and they continued up through tunnels of giant trees with palmed leaves as big as a man.

"There," said Nathan, and he pointed. Along the road, stood a shifty stand erected along the edge of a rocky incline that dropped into the water below. "They sell rum there, straight from the cask, and sometimes, little cakes."

Christine watched it go by, fascinated, and nodded at the woman wearing a small, knitted cap who was minding the business. "It's almost like a fair," she said in surprise.

"Yes, the laws are different here," agreed Nathan, "but as you can see there is as much to be changed as there is in the states."

She tore her gaze from the fluttering long grass along the roadside and turned to examine the bright blue sea over his shoulder. "War?" she guessed in a tired voice.

"Someday. For now, Britain has taken over much of the French colonies with its revolution business on the continent, which makes it more dangerous for me. There are some Union Jacks still unfriendly towards us colonists despite the years that have passed, and there is always one dispute or another over the islands, leaving the people caught in the middle of it all."

"Dreadful," she mumbled.

"Yes. I would dare to guess it will take another century or an uprising before all men are free—at least in the Indies. Who knows for our Republic and its permissive practices."

The sandy dirt road began to climb into steeper paths that snaked up the island's heights like a ribbon. Christine shook off the gloom and gave a small chuckle with each jarring bounce of the carriage. It rocked far to the left and then over to the right, carrying them back and forth up into the hills. They passed, as promised, a plantation set up on a low hill beyond a high stone wall. The long, one-story house had a low roof with a lovely porch framed by columns and scrollwork. It stood up high on a set of stone pilings that looked much like legs. A sugar distillery rose like cones before its face, and workers roamed back and forth like dark, busy bees. Christine realized with a start it was all nothing more than a prison. Sugar was not a luxury here.

As they drove up into the island's heights, the carriage driver seemed determined that his passengers should slide back and forth or be pressed together like pickled eggs in a jar. Christine could not help but feel a rush of elation each time the Captain's warm side pressed into hers or he took her elbow and held her tight. Once, he looped his arms through hers and took her hand to keep her from pitching out the other side.

It amazed her—his touch and the feelings it gave her. It was more than a pleasing tingle like she felt dancing with a handsome Talbot twin. Rather, it was more of a cannonade of pleasure that made her heart bloom and flutter down into her belly. Their companionship made her feel almost giddy, and yet she felt comfortable and safe at the same time. No wonder Matty esteemed him so.

Without the crew lurking around, Nathan seemed more comfortable and happier to be with her. He'd long dropped the mask of irritation he'd first worn when he realized he'd have a woman aboard his ship and in his business. How happy she was that they were friends now and that this was the last time he'd bypass authorities in the ports. Most importantly, he cared for her brother's safety as much as she did.

"What are you staring at?" laughed Nathan. He touched his head which had lost its hat. "Has my hair blown straight up?"

She grinned, pretending to study the breadfruit trees he'd pointed out. "I'm only happy you are no longer angry with me, Captain Butler, and I'm enjoying this tour."

"Yes, I see," he countered as a carriage wheel dropped into a large hole and the entire vehicle almost turned on its side.

"Oh," cried Christine with a groan, and they both burst into laughter as they held on for their lives.

"Careful, Mr. Smith, if you please," called Nathan as the carriage righted itself.

Christine could only chuckle again. His handsome face and broad smile and good humor made the day feel glorious, even if they tipped over.

"Pardon, Captain, and here are the falls, sir," called Mr. Smith over his shoulder.

"Oh, yes," said Nathan with renewed excitement. The dirt road, now more a path with little room for their carriage, turned sharply into a grove of tall, narrow trees. Beyond them, nature thickened into a jungle-looking forest. "This will do," called Nathan, and Christine eyed him with curiosity.

He gave her a secretive look that reminded her of the first time she'd spied him in the marsh, and she quieted. Was he taking her to a smuggler's meeting place? What was he thinking putting her in such danger!

The driver pulled the exhausted horse to a stop and then jumped down from the seat. He helped Christine out then turned to see to the animal. Nathan picked up a canvas bag from the back and motioned for her to follow.

Leaving the horse and driver behind, Christine walked with some trepidation into the cool shade of the trees. Small ferns and stubby sprouts of exotic flowers diverged to reveal a narrow, sandy footpath. She stopped once, mesmerized by an enormous toad. "It hardly looks real."

"Cane toad." Nathan tried to catch it, but it hopped away, and she was glad the ugly thing escaped. She followed his broad back until they came upon a tiny stream that seemed to come from nowhere. In the distance, the wind made a loud *shooshing* sound that became louder as they followed the trickling water uphill.

She tried not to stare at the man in front of her. His tall, muscled form made her wonder why she had not allowed herself to admit he was dashingly beautiful—much more handsome than the fair and wealthy gentlemen of her acquaintance.

The air seemed to roar around them like the ocean and curiosity got the better of her. Christine hurried to Nathan's side and peered ahead. He caught her hand in his and led her around a leaning tree. She stopped in her tracks, aware of the jolt of heat that shot up her arm when their fingers met.

In a secluded clearing, a pile of towering dark rocks was stacked this way and that as if by some unseen heavenly hand. A small stream poured over them and crashed down into a large pool at their feet. The noise she'd heard had been a waterfall with the clearest water she'd ever seen. Through the streams of water raining over the falls, she spied a small cave and gasped. "What is this place?" Beside her, Nathan chuckled.

Flowers grew around the edges of the pool, and the air shined with drops that made a thin rainbow over the water. Christine rushed to the edge and saw that it wasn't deep; at least it didn't look so. There were no fish, just pebbles and sand and water as blue as heaven.

"Nathan!" she exclaimed, hoping he was not offended by her address.

He laughed at her awe. "Welcome to Anya's pool."

Christine could not tear her gaze away from the bubbling water. "I've never seen anything like it."

"And you won't," agreed Nathan, "not in Savannah to be sure."

She put a hand on her chest to calm her heart.

"Come here." Nathan led her around the water's edge, and to her delight, scooped her up into his arms so that she did not wet her riding boots. He carried her through water up to his knees to set her on a dry boulder in the pool.

"Who's Anya?" Christine asked as he climbed up beside her.

"It's a legend."

"So was Alligator George. So tell me," she demanded over the sound of falling water.

Nathan leaned back on his hands. The overhead branches of a tree cast a pleasant shade over their boulder, and she folded her legs up beneath her petticoats.

"Anya," said Nathan, leaning close to Christine to speak in her ear, "was a blue-eyed, smoke-skinned maiden from Trinidad. She escaped a life of servitude by stowing away on a fishing boat. A young fisherman found her and tried to keep her hidden, but the crew discovered her, and they threw her off within a swim's reach of St. William.

Christine widened her eyes. "What about sharks?"

He held up a hand. "She was a strong swimmer, many of the island girls are, and she made her way to one of the many lagoons around the island."

Christine leaned in.

"No one saw her come ashore, and afraid her masters would search the Indies for her, she crept high into the jungle until she found this little pool with clear, fresh water." He waved his hand around presenting it to her again. "See, there are breadfruit and mango trees and plenty of shade. Coconuts grow down on the beaches and could be gathered at night."

"Madame Bellerose gave me a mango," Christine informed him. "It's delicious, but I couldn't live up here."

Nathan motioned toward the cave. "She slept in the cave by day, and by night she tiptoed down to the shore to watch for the young fisherman who promised to come back. His face haunted her dreams, and his cries when they threw her overboard gave her hope that she wouldn't have to live out the rest of her days in hiding for long."

When he fell quiet, Christine asked, "Did he come back?"

"Well," said Nathan with a serious dip of his chin, "Elias was forced to go back to Trinidad, but he worried and dreamed about Anya, too. He'd admired her in the village and had watched her in the sugar cane many times, and because of that, he felt like he'd failed her. As soon as he was able, and it took months, he purchased a small boat of his own using all of his savings, and sailed back in search of the small island the fishermen called St. William."

"Did he find her?" Anxious impatience flooded through Christine as she looked around the beautiful scenery and tried to imagine living here. She found it peaceful, but lonely.

"Elias was caught in a storm and had to abandon his quest. After it passed, he was picked up by pirates and forced to sail with them for two long years."

Christine gasped in disappointment, and Nathan pressed his lips together in a line. "When he did escape and find his way to St. William much later, he searched the island from the shore to the hilltops until he discovered this crystal blue falls."

"And?"

He shook his head then whispered into her ear: "He found Anya in the cave curled up into a pile of banana leaves. She'd died of a broken heart."

Christine jerked away and shook off the warm pleasure of feeling his breath on her ear. "She died?" she exclaimed, nearly shouting over the falls.

Nathan gave her a teasing grin. "But look, see the water? It never ran blue until Anya died here. The island folk swore it was just another fountain of water, as sandy and green as the plants around it, until Elias lost his blue-eyed beauty."

Eyes watering, Christine looked away, but Nathan continued. "It was her tears, you see, that turned it blue. 'Blue as Anya's eyes' they say around here these days." He stopped and gave Christine a triumphant smile.

"That's dreadful," she complained. With a frown, she crossed her arms. "Why didn't Elias come sooner? He could have jumped in when the fishermen threw her overboard."

Nathan shrugged. "Men are like that," he mused. "It takes a while for them to understand what's in their hearts."

"Well, he was a fool," snapped Christine. She swallowed down a knot in her throat and gave a pout. He hadn't shifted away since he'd broken *her* heart by whispering the story in her ear.

"Tragic," he said, his eyes gleaming. "I'm sure he wanted to spare her but in that moment he didn't recognize his own heart—or his courage."

Christine stared. She liked Nathan's apology, but she was mesmerized by his gaze. It was as blue as the pristine waters of Anya's pool, framed by dark lashes, and inches from her face. She could smell the tart scent of lime as she glanced down at his full lips close enough to brush her own. Her breath caught in her chest, paralyzing her with trepidation—and to her surprise—a burning, hungry hope.

When she looked up through her lashes into Nathan's eyes, her heart dropped into her lap at his intense and steady stare. If was as if he felt the same way and wanted the same thing. Her pulse began to strum in her ears, as slowly, moving like a dream, he moved his face toward hers and planted a pert kiss on the tip of her nose.

"Come on, lovely girl," he said, jumping up and breaking the spell. "Madame Bellerose will be wondering why we are not home for dinner." He grinned at his joke as he helped Christine to her feet. The water splashing into the pool sprinkled through the air.

Christine looked up at the brilliant sky through the trees and let the water's spray hit her face. She needed it to cool down; to wash away the red she felt in her cheeks; to rinse away the distressing fact that she had looked into the eyes of the most handsome man she'd ever known and wanted him to kiss her, and that he'd kissed her on the nose like a kitten.

The disappointment felt like someone had tossed a bucket of water over a single, flickering flame. Her hands and the crooks of her elbows were damp and not from Anya's waters. Christine prayed Nathan had not noticed she'd felt something blazing and hopeful, and that he'd dowsed it out with his brotherly affection.

NATHAN TOSSED AND TURNED until he crawled out of bed before dawn. A late night supper with one of the traders on the island had dragged on into the night, and he'd allowed it, welcoming the glasses of claret and later, strong rum, to erase the smoldering feelings a simple carriage ride had lit inside of him. He'd almost forgotten he could have such passionate feelings until the heroic and meddling Christine Fryer had crept into his life.

He sat up on the bed to squeeze back an aching headache and the whispering thoughts that tempted him to consider a future with a young woman like her.

"First of all," he mumbled, stomping over to the washstand to scrub his face, "she's Mathew's sister." Rubbing his eyes, he reached for a cloth. "Second of all," he said into the cloth, "she's a Fryer—a very rich Fryer—and the near-fiancée of Richard Hawthorne." He wadded up the material and threw it into a corner of the room.

Walking over to the gritty shutters with a view of the shop next door, he watched an enormous spider in an outside corner spin its web. *Third of all*, he thought, *she is a woman, after all, at a marriageable age and that kind of catch never works out*. He thought of Priscilla Blakemore. It was providence he hadn't settled for her; he'd have ended up like his father, crossed in love and wishing for death.

He thought about his sweet stepmother. He'd loved her as a mother of sorts; at least an older sister. She deserved the love he felt for her, he admitted, but he hadn't let it drive him mad.

Frowning, he picked up the pair of breeches he'd worn aboard the *Siren* the first day in port and pulled them on, hoping the shirt he'd sent to be washed was cleaner than it looked. Madame Bellerose kept her husband's lodging rooms clean and charged a fair rate, but her laundering skills were wanting.

Determined to forget about the ridiculous moment when he'd kissed Christine on the nose, Nathan packed up his things and sent them downstairs. He'd take a horse back to the harbor to see that the *Siren* was ready for departure and that the money from his trading—both legal and smuggled—was locked away under Mr. Walker's protection.

He did not have Isaac with him now and would have to trust the crew. They'd made a pact, the lot of them, to do their business above the board now and to never rat one another out.

He hoped they could be trusted. If they made it into Savannah without any problems, they would be free to go on with their lives if everyone stayed quiet.

Nathan scurried down the stairs, pushing away the guilt he felt for leaving Christine behind. He'd make sure she was fed and dressed and had a carriage to the harbor. One of the crew could escort her up the gang-board. He would be busy, he imagined, or he planned to be, so that he would only greet her and see that she was made comfortable as they readied to sail.

The strong feelings that had emerged for her at the waterfall had been brewing for some time. Still, they'd caught him off his guard. While sitting alone with her at the pool, all of the admiration and attraction for her had escaped his locked up heart and the iron bars of protection fell away.

He'd been hypnotized by her round eyes—as silver as the moon—and had almost melted into her and planted a kiss on her little red mouth. Luckily, he'd caught himself, but the end result had left him looking like a fool. He imagined she felt relieved. She was as kind to him as she was to Hawthorne, he told himself. Her dipping and nodding to the gentlemen crowd were only for her father's sake.

Nathan stood in the street with his mind quivering like pudding until a boy from the inn brought him a weary-looking nag. Nathan calmed it with a few soft words and a piece of sugar cane. Once the old horse relaxed, he mounted it and rode down to the harbor. His things would follow with Christine's meager belongings she'd collected on their journey.

The early sun stretched across a cloud of pillows like a woman in her nightdress as a skiff rowed him out to the moored *Siren*. He climbed aboard to find his men lined up and ready for inspection. The weather glass showed promise. Perhaps the journey home would not only end safely but without poor weather as well.

He was just short of ordering the sails unfurled when Christine was ferried out with the final two crewmen who'd run his last messages. The *Siren* would return in four months' time, he'd promised his suppliers. He'd be an honest merchantman then, legitimate, and a successful and respected Butler at last.

Christine was drawn up over the ship's side in the chair. He forced himself to paste on a polite smile that hid the fact he was falling head over heels for her and hurried over to help her onto the deck. She was watching the water below with suspicious suspense, and he chuckled at her.

"Don't worry," he said, taking her elbow and helping her down. "There's nothing that will get you if you were to fall in."

"It's not the water I'm worried about," she said, tilting back her head to see him from under the brim of her hat, "it's the fall."

"Just land on your feet," he said with a grin, "like a cat."

She smiled and leaned back over the railing to see the water. "I can't believe the color of the Caribbean," she said with adoration. "Every time I look I think it's a dream."

Nathan stepped back and made a show of studying her, forgetting his oath to be nothing more than courteous. "I think a blue-green gown would suit you. If I ever find silk like that I'll be sure to... save it for your brother."

"You mean sell it to my brother," she said with a smirk. The light look in her eyes pricked his heart, and he remembered what he had to do. "Yes," he said, forcing back a smile, "that I do." He proffered his arm and led her to his steward. The old man quickly invited her to retire.

Before she could thank him or say anything else, Nathan turned on his heel as if the ship's needs consumed his every thought. His sudden pivot in body and mood he blamed on necessity, and it pained him, but at least he did not have to see her face. It was best for them both, he realized, if they spent less time together now. After all, they were returning home.

Nathan raised a hand and rested it against the mast as he stared at the stern. Yes, Savannah. Where Miss Christine Fryer would be released by pirates, probably ruined for good, and he would have to pretend to hardly know her. It would only be in passing through his business with her brother.

CHAPTER ELEVEN

C hristine wasn't certain, but she had the unsettling feeling that Nathan was avoiding her. She'd stayed in his quarters until the ship made it out of the harbor and into the sea. On deck, she stayed out of the crew's way and watched St. William shrink in the distance. Nathan stayed at the helm, and not wanting to distract him, she'd returned to her little room and carefully unpacked her things.

There wasn't much. She'd only come with the garments on her back. On the island, the madame had fitted her with the white loose-fitting gown, a pair of sturdy slippers, two hats, one a straw bergère and the other, a quite native wrap. Nathan had ordered her a second set of petticoats, two shifts, and a lovely gown and stomacher in cream linen with blue and red bouquets. He'd assured her Matty would be billed for the inconvenience, so she did not mind accepting it all. But they weren't her greatest treasures.

She had discovered an enormous pink and peach-colored conch shell that looked like it came from Poseidon's lair, a carved coconut with a bird's face, and a beautiful dark stone polished by the grieving waters at Anya's pool. It was almost as dark as onyx—the color of Nathan's hair. How she would treasure that.

The steward brought a message to her at midday inviting her to dinner, and she dined for the first time with Nathan and his wardroom around the long table outside her sleeping quarters. The table was heaped with fish, rice, peppers, and cassava bread. The rum, which she allowed herself to taste since she was among friends anyway, washed all the food down, and she even found herself taking to the limes, sliced and eating them like a native, well, the sailors anyway. Life at sea suited her, Christine decided, and she would have told them all so, except no one asked her any questions.

"Thank you for dinner," she said to Nathan as she realized the men were waiting for her to take her leave. He jumped to his feet, and the others followed suit.

"Thank you for your company, Miss Fryer." He gave her a stiff smile, and she wondered why he did not ask about her day or her thoughts now that she'd explored St. William. True, they'd talked on their walks down to the shore from the inn and on the carriage ride around the island, but he seemed distracted and withdrawn as if what had transpired between them was forgotten.

With a touch of disquiet, Christine strolled the deck alone as the crew took their meals in shifts. She watched the blazing sun bring the sea to a sapphire glow, and when she felt hot and fearful of burning her skin, tiptoed back inside to find the dinner party broken up. She slipped into her quarters alone.

Pacing the cabin and stopping only to peep out of the porthole at the endless blue water, Christine realized there was nothing to do for the oncoming days but sew and read and rest. Then she'd be home.

For a few moments, she allowed herself to think about what would happen when she returned to Savannah, and it made her heart quicken with anxiety. There wasn't a great deal of time to brace herself for the future. Nathan had said they would come up with a story to explain her time away, but she knew in her heart it would come to no good.

There was no way being kidnapped by pirates would ever be forgotten. Her reputation would never be what it was before. The image of Papa's horrified and ashamed face made her shudder. She realized it was likely he would feel it best if she were simply dead.

GUILT IRRITATED NATHAN's conscience until it felt like a pebble in his shoe. He tried not to think about the girl sleeping in his cot. He tried not to imagine her dark hair splayed out on the small pillow or think about the pulse in her swan-like neck moving to the steady rhythm of her dreams.

He squeezed his eyes shut then glanced up at the ratlines overhead. If he turned around, he'd spy Christine at her usual spot between the cabin and rail; making every effort to stay out of the way while she enjoyed the fresh air and scenery.

The day before last, they were followed by a pod of dolphins leapfrogging over the waves in silver rainbows. It'd amused everyone aboard but captivated the innocent young woman. Her delight had been contagious, and when his two men who did the fishing gave him suggestive glances, he shook his head. He couldn't allow for the woman-child to see the beautiful creatures tricked into coming near the hull and then hauled up to become vittles.

Feeling Christine's gaze upon him on occasion, Nathan jumped up the footholds of the mast and climbed until he was beneath the highest yardarm. The wind whipped violently at this height, and it felt glorious. He wondered if he could convince her to climb the mast with him, and he guessed that she'd be tempted if he promised her a safety line.

She was not a reckless thing, but she didn't shrink from adventure. He glanced down at the straw-covered crown of her head. She'd returned to her study of the horizon sensing, it seemed, that he was pulling away from the friendship that had budded on the voyage down and blossomed while in the islands. Perhaps she understood, or at least realized, that anything between them could not be.

The thought sent disappointment washing over him in a gritty wave. Looking out over the royal blue sea, he admitted if he were ever to fall in love like his unfortunate father, a woman such as Christine might do the job. At least, he comforted himself, she was no fraud like Priscilla Blakemore, or desperate like the young ladies he watched throw themselves at Mathew. She was rich, but she wasn't a snob.

With a grunt, he dropped down to the next rope, and his heart did a cartwheel. That rush, the joy of being aloft, was not much different than how he felt when he looked into Christine's eyes, and she gazed back. Dangerous waters.

He climbed down, deciding to spend a few moments with her anyway. He could not avoid her the entire voyage; she'd think him angry or cold, or maybe that he'd only been attentive on the island to keep her content until he could ship her home.

"No dolphins today?" Nathan tried to sound playful.

She seemed surprised that he'd crept up behind her. "Why look, no, but I can't help watching for them now."

He grinned. "They're amusing, aren't they?"

"It's not the same as seeing them from shore," she agreed, "and there were so many."

"You must see a whale while at sea," he told her, leaning over the rail and folding his arms. "Now there is a magical beast."

"Enormous," she agreed. "I've seen a few from the distance when they've been dragged into port. I must say though, nothing will come as close to my affection for the turtles in the island's coves and marshes."

"Yes," he agreed. "Sea turtles. Cursed big things. As big as Blakemore's supper table."

"And his ballroom," laughed Christine. She grinned at her exaggeration, but her eyes looked guarded.

Looking away, Nathan said, "Will you come to dinner again? The men enjoy your company."

"Only because I answer their questions about lumber and honey," she relented.

"They're quite fascinated with beekeeping. I'm impressed with your knowledge of it." Sensing her study, he looked sideways and found a pensive expression on her face.

"Thank you," she said in a quiet rush, "for taking me ashore to see the island. I know I've been a bother," she admitted. "I mean, I suppose it's my fault that—"

He held up his hand to stop her. "No, Christine. It's not your fault at all. If I would have taken better measures, you would never have seen us in the marsh. Bringing you along, well..." He looked away, unable to bear hurting her if it did, "—it was a mistake."

She turned her head so that he could not read her face.

"I should have taken you back home that night and risked setting off late. I could have made excuses if I was spied dawdling close to shore." Nathan took a deep breath when she didn't respond. "Now your future is in ruins and all because of me."

Nathan glanced down at his arms and stared at a sticky, black fleck of tar on his sleeve. The wind billowed across his shirt, but the dark stain did not move. "We will row you ashore when we reach the waterway to our inlet, and you can rest at Clearwater. Then at dawn, my man, Isaac, will ride you into town and say he found you wandering in the marsh. I'll sail up-river and arrive at the docks a day later."

Christine was silent for a time, and he wondered if she understood. He turned to her, and she said, "Yes, of course, Captain Butler, it all makes perfect sense."

"Don't worry about Hawthorne," he said in a rush. He knew her chances of making a match with her father's favorite suitor were now in jeopardy. "He's a good man at heart and won't blame you for any of this business. I'm sure his attentions will be just as... ardent." Nathan almost spat out the last words. They tasted bitter on his tongue.

Christine surprised him by walking away without a word. Fearing her distressed, he followed her into the cabin. "Are you well?" he sputtered from behind her.

She jerked as if he'd yanked her back. Turning slowly, she faced him with a patient smile. "Yes, Captain Butler." She sounded like she was speaking to a stranger, and her gaze skipped around the room like she couldn't bear to look him in the eyes.

Nathan watched a vein pulse in the side of her neck, now tinted pink from too much time in the sun. "I'm not concerned about Mr. Hawthorne at all," she added in a strange tone, then slipped further into the room and shut the door.

Nathan stayed rooted to the boards at his feet. He wondered what she meant by it—she'd claimed to have no intention of marrying the old fellow once before—but now she seemed to have surrendered to it. Her eyes had looked downcast when she'd closed the door, and he thought they had glimmered with tears.

Morose, he plodded back out onto the deck and watched the horizon for more dolphins. Later, Christine did not join them for dinner after all or take any supper later. He was very sorry to learn she'd come down with a headache.

THE SAILS WERE EXCHANGED for canvas of a different color, and a large board painted with the title, *Dragon*, was attached over the *Siren's* name on the stern. Discomfited that she was officially aboard Nathan's pirate ship again, Christine kept to her personal space once they reached the coast. More mending was brought to her room as if Nathan thought it was a gift. He'd practically ordered her to do it in the beginning, but when he saw that she enjoyed it and was quite skilled, it'd become a favor between them.

Christine tossed a tattered waistcoat to her feet. Being confined to her room in the heat of the day had gone from feeling safe to feeling like a prison. Nathan had ignored her for most of the journey home, and now the shores of Georgia were outside her porthole. There was a strange tension over the ship now that Savannah was within reach. She wasn't sure if it was because of her or because the last leg of the voyage was dangerous.

She was apprehensive, too, and lonely. Her unexpected adventure beyond the marsh to the West Indies seemed like something from a fairytale. Her real life would continue in Savannah, but would it ever be the same?

A knock on the door made her jump. She'd skipped dinner again with another poor excuse, but she could not bear to sit at Nathan's table like they were scarcely acquainted. She pulled open the hatch and stepped back, surprised to see him there. He had tucked his shirt into his dark breeches and tied a scarlet sash around his trim waist. His hair was combed back and a small, dark shadow on his chin trimmed neatly. He gave her a faint but sincere smile that she hadn't seen in many weeks.

"We missed you this afternoon," he said. He held out his hand. "The sun is setting over the coastline. Would you like to watch it sink into the treetops of Georgia?"

"We're almost home?"

He nodded and reached his hand further out, entreating her to join him. "We'll reach the inlet most likely by tonight."

That meant maneuvering up the waterways. Christine took a nervous breath. "I thought we had a few more days." She realized Nathan's hand still hung in the air, and so she accepted it. He was being more personable than usual. She'd already determined to put him out of her heart, for he'd not only kidnapped her, but it, too.

They stepped out into a glorious breeze that made her shiver. The weather had turned in the Americas. It would not stay summer forever like it did in the Indies.

He tucked her hand into the crook of his arm, and her breath caught in her throat when his fingers brushed against her skin. She looked away and stared at the sun giving way to dusk.

"I've ordered a light supper, enough, I think, to fill you up and make it through the night to come."

"I'm sure it will." She bit her lip and hoped her tone sounded careless but gracious. They moved over to the rail and looked across the span of darkening water. Bubbling, gray foam flounced across the waves like swishing lace hems.

"I hoped to have a moment with you," said Nathan in a low tone, "to tell you how much I enjoyed our time together, Christine."

He stopped and cleared his throat, but if it was an invitation to meet his stare, she would not accept it. It was already beginning to hurt—the separation that must come. That he should have the power to wound her so was humbling and chilling.

"I—I—"

She glanced over, surprised to hear him stuttering like a nervous boy. He let out a whoosh of breath and gave a soft chuckle. "The thing is, Christine, I hope you have not found me too distracted or unkind." He shook his head a little as if frustrated with his words. "What I mean is, I've enjoyed our time together, and I look forward to seeing you in Savannah."

Christine wondered if he could hear her heart beating like a drum. Did he mean to call? She allowed herself to meet his steady gaze and found him staring.

"Under the proper circumstances, of course," he said. "I hope we will always be at least... friends."

Her heart dropped like a stone into her riding boots. She hadn't realized it'd risen to her throat. Knowing he waited for a response, she forced down the thick lump of disappointment, although it hurt. "Friends," she whispered in agreement. Her heart cracked into shards.

A strange cry echoed overhead, and Nathan jerked his head up. His prolonged stare made Christine look, too. It wasn't an annoying gull like she presumed. She tried to replay the sound in her head but was distracted by the crew—every man on deck—who'd frozen in mid-step.

The voice echoed again, and it was from the crow's nest. She looked south over the stern. A twinge of concern poked her in the chest, and she looked back at Nathan. His jaw slackened, his eyes rounded, and his lips parted as if trying to draw a breath.

"What is it?" she asked, sensing fear in the air.

"Company!" someone called from the yardarm, and the man beside her jumped into action. After shouting orders, he snatched Christine by the elbow and pushed her toward the cabin. "Go, now," he told her. The wind stirred over his head as more sails were loosed and caught the breeze.

"What is it?" she cried as she dashed for her quarters. "Pirates?" She shuddered at the recollection of some of the crew's stories. Were they not even safe posing as Alligator George?

"No," Nathan snapped, "Americans!" and he dashed to the helm.

Pulse pounding, Christine rushed into her room, shut the hatch tight, and barricaded it like it would keep out an army. She hurried over to the cot and fell onto it, puffing to catch her breath. Waning light through the porthole lit up the small sea chest holding all her treasures. Her palms were wet with perspiration, and she wiped them on her gown.

Someone had caught up with Nathan, and he was carrying undeclared cargo on the books. Worse, they were under a black flag. And she was supposed to have been captured by pirates.

THE DECISION TO FLEE was easy but dreadful. Nathan felt the blame of the men over the excitement of the chase. They could not fight. The risk of being boarded or sunk with Christine on board was too great. Even if he could charm his way out of the ship being searched and explain away questions as to the timing of his arrival in port, there was no excuse for having Christine Fryer on board—not one that would satisfy her family—and worse, she knew their entire operation. Would she keep it secret if she were questioned?

There was nothing they could do but pretend they had not spotted the coastal gunship and then make a run for it in the dark. It looked like a familiar privateer. Nathan stood on the con with every muscle in his body taut. The night was coming on, but not fast enough.

He considered his options. He could drop Christine into a longboat and leave her in Mr. Walker's charge. How he'd explain the man missing from the ship once they reached Savannah, he did not know. That was a problem. He shook his head.

By the glow of the now violet-colored sky, he watched the schooner appear to gain. The *Siren* was heavy with cargo, their pursuer light with nothing but minimal supplies and her guns. He thanked his maker that the moon would not be full tonight, not even by half, as he'd planned their landing with some intelligence.

But he hadn't wanted to see an American privateer. Any other time they'd seen sails had either been excusable or he'd lofted the colors of a pirate, but he'd never been caught so close to the inlet before—so near the haunts of Alligator George.

Nathan's heart hammered as his minds swirled with options. There was no time to reach the waters that streamed in and out of Sandpiper. He would have to throw his cargo overboard and say they'd been boarded by pirates. The tale would match, too, with Alligator George now sighted by the Americans. The problem was Christine. The only answer made him feel faint, but what else could he do?

With a frown, he ordered the ship to cruise closer to the shoals which frightened his man with the lead line. "Send for Miss Fryer," Nathan said next in a strangled voice when they were within sight of the inlet's entrance. The bosun made it so, and soon she arrived escorted by a serious and drawn Mr. Walker.

Taking a deep breath, Nathan announced, "Over she goes, Mr. Walker, but you'll have to stay."

"What?" Christine sounded confused.

The first mate raised a brow in the dim lantern light. "You don't want me to row her in?"

Nathan shook his head as his chest sank at the look of fear on Christine's face. He pointed into the darkness at the nearby sand bar that looked almost black in the night.

"See there, Miss Fryer," he said in a cold, formal voice, "I'm going to put you over in our smallest boat and give you an oar.

Paddle to there for the night, and you can wade over to the shore by morning."

"No, you can't leave me here." The look on her face was of shock although her voice was calm, hushed, and tense.

"We cannot stop even to unload the ship. You'll have to make your own way home alone."

"But, Nathan," she cried and a smudge of fear tainted her voice, "you can't just throw me overboard."

"It's no different a plan than we had to begin with, except now you go without Mr. Walker, and you have a little further to go."

She gaped like he'd ordered her shot, and he watched her bosom heave up and down. He let down his guard. "There's nothing to it, Christine, especially for a girl like you. You're clever and brave, and you know your way through the marsh. Follow the beach north until you reach the channel, and it will lead you inland into the marsh at Sandpiper Point. From there," he took a breath, realizing he was speaking so fast he was breathless, "well, you know your way home. It's only a day's walk."

She narrowed her eyes at him, and in the darkness their color was lost. "I can't go that far alone. It's nighttime. And the water, what if it's deep?" Her voice trembled, and the feelings and hopes he'd stowed tightly away cracked from the pressure into deep, jagged fissures.

"It's not. I know the place." He forced himself to sound confident—and aloof. Perhaps he even sounded blameful. "Mr. Walker," he repeated as he brushed by her and she took a step back, "send her over."

"No!" cried Christine.

He didn't turn back, he couldn't bear to. The bosun stood by with her sea chest at the ready. "Don't," he called to him and pointed. "She can't take that now. Throw her things into the water, and get her off the ship."

There was a cry of frustration, and he could have sworn she cursed his name, but maybe he imagined it. Box and pulley whirled as the petite boat was launched holding the young woman hatless and caught off guard. She was gasping with fear so loudly he could hear her from the helm.

Christine called his name one more time after the boat smacked into the shallow water, but Nathan forced his mind back to the *Dragon*. There was not a minute to waste. They raised their sails and backed into the deep before racing away into the night. He altered their course for the Atlantic in a way that would bring them straight into the mouth of the Savannah River—without their pirate colors and an American hunter searching for them under the stars.

CHAPTER TWELVE

Christine awakened with a jerk. A chuckling flock of gulls circled overhead like they'd found something to eat. She groaned as she sat up, and every muscle and bone rebelled against the movement. The sun had crept halfway above the line of horizon, and a soft peach light glowed over the beach. Tall sea grasses rippled *good morning* across the dunes in the distance.

Had she slept? It couldn't have been more than a few hours. She looked down at her damp petticoats and the wadded up gown she'd tried to sleep on in the bottom of the boat. It was more a log. Nathan Butler had tossed her overboard into a tiny, unsteady craft and sent her off into the night. She clenched her jaw. She'd been too frightened to cry last night.

More birds fluttered by, making noises that pierced the peaceful swish of waves lapping the shoreline. It was rather flat, littered with pebbles and broken pieces of seashells. Christine allowed herself to remember how it felt to walk through the groves of island palm trees and study the crystal green-blue water with Nathan at her side. A painful bubble swelled up in her chest. The time had meant nothing to him. As soon as he had the chance, he'd thrown her overboard without a backward glance.

Angry, she stiffened and looked around. She tried to stand, and it rocked the boat, but she caught herself before tipping out into the sand. It'd been a dreadful cradle, but it carried her to the nearby shoal after she was cast off the ship.

As soon as her eyes had adjusted, and she realized she could dimly see the shore, she'd dragged the boat over the sandbar and paddled for land praying there wouldn't be sharks or other dreadful things between her and safety. Luckily, the sea had been calm and did not slam into the beach like it did in so many other places.

Christine searched the horizon. There was no sign of the *Siren*. No evidence of the *Dragon*. She saw no fishing boats either and realized she was quite alone. Nathan had said she must walk north along the shore until she found the streaming waterway, and it would lead her into the marsh.

"At least it's not raining," she mumbled and made an effort to comb her fingers through her hair before twisting it into a knot. She shook out her petticoats, slid on her old riding boots, and straightened her gown over her shoulders. The stomacher was long lost.

With a sense of wonder at her circumstances and numb to the possibilities of what would come, she plodded along the shore for what seemed like ages, winding her way through the dunes and sharp grass until she saw the mouth of the river. After resting for a time inside a copse of trees, she rolled down her torn stockings to cool her legs and trudged along the banks that grew thick before flattening out. The heavy trees thinned a bit and soon the open marsh spread out before her with giant cedar trees thrusting heavenward.

A few times, the tunes of the gulping frogs and soprano crickets made her pause, and she scanned the wetland for alligators waiting to gobble her up. But there was nothing, just her old familiar friends—creaking crickets, buzzing bees, and the occasional splash of water from a creeping crane or timid turtle. The air felt cold the night before, and she'd shivered for hours, but now the sun was reheating the marsh, and it would soon feel like late summer although autumn was near.

When she reached the inlet, Christine trudged through the muck until she reached the cottonwood grove. Her mouth was parched, and her stomach grumbled for something to eat. The pain Nathan had caused her simmered into a fit of roiling anger. He'd sent her off with no water, little food, and nothing to protect her from the elements. When she thought about how much further it was to town, she wanted to cry. But after a time, the breeze stirred in the trees, and a boll of cottony clouds rolled across the sky blocking out the sun. She forced herself forward with a surprising burst of determination. It was not much further now.

Missing Janus, Christine trekked along the worn animal trail the gelding knew well until she reached the open dirt road that led to Savannah's outskirts. She walked along the dusty red road feeling much like a gypsy, both hoping for a buggy or farmer to come along, but at the same time dreading it.

As the blisters on her toes became unbearable, she slipped off her boots and walked down the center of the lane with rubbery legs wishing she still had the slippers from Madame Bellerose. Nathan had told his officer to throw her treasures overboard. Her new clothes, her seashells, everything. She hated him for it.

Sweat trickled down her back, along her arms, and straight down the back of her knees. At long last, when she had almost quit searching the distant horizon, the outline of Savannah's first structures could be seen. She stopped and wrapped strips of petticoat hem around her feet and forced them back into her shoes. It made her steps slower and more unsteady, but she wobbled along determined to continue until she fainted.

It was a fisherman and his wife who found her in the late, heavy afternoon. When she stumbled toward their wagon rolling and shaking along like old bones, the woman hopped down and called out to her if she was ill. Christine waited until the kind fishwife wrapped a shawl around her shoulders before she gave her name, and when the husband helped her into the back with its stinking barrels and fish guts, she curled up and pretended to swoon.

She did not open her eyes again until the wagon stopped, and she heard Abigail and the cook. They were standing on the steps of home with their hands clasped to their bosoms. Both of them cried out when Christine sat up. She made it halfway up the steps to the door with their arms around her before her trembling legs gave way. Defeated, she sank to the ground and began to sob so deeply that she could not catch her breath.

NATHAN SAILED THE *Dragon* back to sea under cover of night, and with Walker at his side, used the stars to come about and take them back toward the Savannah River by morning. The lookouts stayed up through the night, watching for dim lanterns that signaled a sneaking ship, and the crew replaced the *Dragon's* canvas with the *Siren's* colors.

After pacing the deck for hours, Nathan decided if he was to become a legitimate merchantman, he must cut all ties to his smuggling and the lurking legend of Alligator George.

"Mr. Walker," he called, and his first mate strode across the deck in the dim starlight.

"Sir?" His voice sounded tired; they all were. The first signs of dawn were just a few short hours away.

"It's time to drop the boards—the *Dragon's* name, the paint, and all of her canvas, into the sea."

"Are you sure?"

"Yes," said Nathan. "I have no intention to sail again under the disguise, and this will end the temptation once and for all."

"But I think we lost them, Captain. The ship has probably turned back to search along the coast."

"And they'll find nothing. They'll search the rivers and inlets first; a pirate would never sail directly into Savannah."

Walker hesitated, and Nathan understood. "It's been a good masquerade and a bit of fun, but it's time to let the story die. We've never attacked a ship, but the rumors will grow, and soon we'll be as feared as Blackbeard. It does us no service if we're to start sailing honestly now. It's better to let it go."

"Yes, sir," said Walker, but still he hesitated, looking around to see if anyone was in earshot. "And Miss Fryer, do you think she will tell?"

"She won't." Nathan had tried to put her from his mind all night—tried not to show how he was wracked with fear for her safety. "I'll contact her brother as soon as we arrive. If she has not been found, I'll ride out to Clearwater and search the marsh myself.

Mr. Walker nodded in agreement. "Count me in."

Nathan reached out and shook his hand. "I thank you for it." He prayed she had not done anything foolish and drowned herself.

"Don't worry, Captain," said Walker as if reading his mind. "She can ride a horse and take care of herself in the marsh. It wasn't but a stone's throw to the shoals, and there weren't any strong currents. I'm sure she's back to shore by now and is halfway home."

Nathan looked up at the stars. "Let's hope so." She'd been furious with him as she'd been lowered into the water. Hopefully, the rage would fuel her far enough to find her way back to Savannah.

The crew set the ship on a course to their home port, and Nathan retired to his cabin and books. He made a few changes on the ledgers, hoping his numbers and cargo appeared to match up, and made a few convenient smudges to hide the excess merchandise he could not make himself toss overboard with Christine.

By dawn, the steward brought him fresh coffee, and he drank two steaming cups before retiring to wash up for the port and River Street. The mouth of the river lay just ahead, and he wanted to look presentable when he made his way down the docks to learn if Miss Christine Fryer had lately been recovered by pirates.

A thumping knock made him jump as he slipped the clean shirt over his head.

"Captain Butler."

He opened it with a jumpy heart. It was the bosun. "The spotter sees sails."

Nathan's heart stopped cold. "American?"

"Aye, sir. The same beast as yesterday."

"How far are we from land?"

"Sighted at last bells."

Nathan locked his jaws together so that he did not sigh aloud. Instead, he swallowed and said, "Stay the course. Inform me if they signal to lay to"—meaning to alert him if it was an American watchman cruising the area. He could not bring himself to say "board." They'd never been caught or questioned at sea. He could not believe his final jaunt home from the Indies might end this way.

It wasn't long before the murmur of voices on deck became quieter and sounded tenser. Nathan finished shaving, rehearsed his story in his mind—one all of the crew knew by heart—and strode out pretending to feel confident and carefree. He bounded up to the helm, had a word with the navigator, and leaned back on the taffrail watching the distant ship approach.

She flew American colors and moved fast. "The *Hornet*," muttered Nathan to himself. He let a groan escape. She was speedy and light and took her assignment protecting Georgia's coastline seriously. Judging from the masts and sails, it was indeed the very ship that had pursued them through the night.

Nathan's chest continued its nervous drumbeat as he wiped his hands on his coat. As the schooner approached, he studied her guns. He did not carry many—he was a smuggler, not a pirate. He'd flee before fighting.

The officer aboard the *Hornet* shouted for them to lie to, and Nathan dropped a bow anchor and let *Siren* bob up and down on the water. He waited with feigned patience for them to board, kept his face impassive, and nodded at Mr. Walker to carry on as planned.

Four men climbed over the rail, and Walker welcomed them. Since their captain had chosen to stay aboard, Nathan nodded across the water at him. Wilson, he thought his name was, and then he waited to be approached by the officers.

"Captain," said the officer in a cool tone.

Nathan answered his clipped bow. The *Siren's* men on deck were put back to work as if they owed no respect or allegiance to the visitors, and they did not mind them at all.

"You are in-bound to Savannah, I presume," said the first lieutenant.

Nathan raised a shoulder as if the man was stupid. Walker cleared his throat. "We are returning from the Indies as is our usual routine."

"Yes," said the officer in a slow tone, glancing around the deck. "Your second trip this year?"

"Third," enunciated Nathan making it clear he would not be tripped up or tricked into saying something that could be used against him.

"Well, I am happy to see you safe and sound," said the officer agreeably. He nodded at Walker, and Nathan realized they were familiar with one another.

"We hoped to reach port by this evening," said Walker as if Nathan was not there.

"I see." The officer glanced over the water at his captain. "Might I have a quick tour of the ship? Check your books?"

"Your captain doesn't want to come aboard?"

The lieutenant turned his piercing gaze on him. "We're in a bit of a hurry, Captain Butler," he admitted. "We had quite the chase last night, but our prey eluded us in the outer banks."

Nathan nodded at the schooner. "She sails well along the coast, does she not?"

"Yes, but we didn't want to risk the shoals in the dead of night."

Nathan raised a brow. "It must have been a chase indeed and quite close."

"Quite," agreed the officer. He glanced toward his vessel then lowered his voice. "The *Dragon*, you see..." He raised his brows for emphasis. "I saw the stern myself. We know she's north of Darien unless she turned during the night."

"Upon my word," said Nathan like a housewife. He glanced at Walker and pretended to look concerned. "We are lucky to have made it to Savannah in one piece after all."

"Did you see her?" asked the *Hornet's* lieutenant. The officers crowded around the helm, their ears pricked up and distracted from their original intent to search the ship.

"I don't dare sail my ship so near the hammocks and shoals," said Nathan in a serious tone, "not with pirates and privateers up my craw. I prefer the open waters, but we did spot a trio of ships three days back, British I believe, but lost them on the horizon."

"Heading northeast," agreed Walker.

"But no other ships?"

Nathan set his mouth in a tight line and shrugged. "We did not."

"Thank the heavens," mumbled Walker for effect. He glanced over his shoulder as if unhurried. "You have time to see the ship?"

"Just a look."

Walker took the officers and two guards below deck to see the goods and note the minimal firepower, for a pirate ship would be loaded. After a brusque tour, he escorted the first lieutenant to the cabin where Nathan offered them drink then pulled open the books and showed his stamps from St. William and a quick look at the ledgers. The man obviously wasn't interested in taking inventory to make sure the numbers aligned.

"This ship you saw," probed Nathan, while the lieutenant glanced over the pages, "did she fire?"

"Hmm? No." The officer looked up. "We gave chase although the light was fading, but our spotter has good eyes. He saw the name on the stern—bright and clear and boasting, and we chased her into the darkness as she set a course toward the coastline."

"She probably hid in an inlet," mused Nathan.

"Yes," said the lieutenant in disgust, "and we sailed right by." He glanced anxiously out the porthole and shut the ledger, then gave the crews' names on the books a precursory examination.

"All aboard," Nathan reassured him.

The officer thanked him, rounded up his men, and Nathan saluted the captain with a respectable volley. He waited for the *Hornet* to veer away and head south toward the inlets in search of her prey.

When the ship was out of sight, he pretended to observe the crew continue their usual routines before walking back to his cabin with a satisfied smirk. "It's a blessed thing we dumped the sails and evidence," Walker murmured as Nathan gave him the helm. He nodded with confidence as if he'd never worried at all.

When he shut the door behind him, he collapsed onto the cot and put his hands on his face. His shirt was soaked with sweat, and his stomach clenched as tight as a drum. He drew in a deep breath and let it out in a slow stream. Nearly discovered. Yet they'd managed to convince them otherwise. He had far more cargo aboard than was recorded in the ledgers. They should have dumped it, too.

Encouraging his muscles to relax and his heartbeat to ease, Nathan rolled over onto his side. He'd been awake for two days straight, and his eyes felt like prickly weights.

He closed them and inhaled, and the sweet scent of Christine filled his senses. He lifted up his head and stared, but it was only the pillow under his head—the one she'd slept on for weeks. It smelled like her, floral and sweet, and another arrow pierced his heart. He would not be able to bear it if she'd come to any harm in the marsh.

He should have kissed her, he realized and kissed her good, at the waterfall and before he sent her overboard into the night. He should have shown her he was more than fond of her and that she was more than an inconvenience. She was, he realized, the most beautiful creature he'd ever known, and he wanted to be with her, not as a friend, he realized with diminishing chagrin, but as more. Much more.

His father's memory rose in his thoughts, and he let a faint smile creep across his tired face. "And now it's me," he mumbled, knowing the time had come. Life could not keep a heart barricaded forever, and that's what she'd done without even knowing. Christine had sailed straight into a smuggler's heart without even trying, and he wouldn't let her go.

CHRISTINE SPENT THREE days in bed after scrubbing herself in a bath and changing into a comfortable, worn shift. Abigail had combed out her hair and plaited it back into a loose braid then covered her with a light quilt. The maid only returned in the mornings with trays of tea and broths.

Christine was not ill, but she let them think so. Papa visited once, his face drawn and flushed. The doctor examined and questioned her, but she remained evasive. Soon, the story would come out, but it would not be wholly true, and this weighed on her.

A knock at the door turned her head from the window where she was musing while propped up on soft, comfortable pillows, two and three deep. "Yes?"

It was less of a croak now. Abigail opened the door. "You have a visitor, Miss Christine. Miss Fenton is here."

Christine gave a small dip of her head. When Dolly marched into the room, rather stiff and pensive, Christine smiled at her with relief and patted the bed. "Come here, my sweet friend," she said.

Dolly needed no other encouragement. She darted across the rug and threw herself into Christine's arms. "Oh, Christine," she cried and crumbled into tears. "I thought you were dead. Gone forever. Eaten by alligators or stolen by pirates."

"Or worse," murmured Christine into her hair.

Dolly pulled back, her face crumpled in distress. "What could be worse? Is it true then? Pirates? The whole town is saying so. Was it Alligator George?" Her entire body trembled at the horror of the idea.

Christine forced herself to speak. "Yes, pirates, but not a bad lot. I mean," she added, "I was treated well for the most part."

"And you escaped?"

She nodded again, letting Dolly search her eyes for only a moment. "They stopped in an inlet, and I ran away until I was just walking and walking and walking." That was mostly true.

Dolly put her hands to her pale throat. "How we prayed for you—and mourned, too. To have lost my closest and best friend." She hugged her again, and Christine closed her eyes to fight back the regret. She had truly caused everyone so much pain.

"Your papa," said Dolly, pulling away but reaching for her hand to hold, "he's beside himself, I'm sure."

"Are you?" Christine couldn't keep the dismissive tone from her voice. It seemed Papa wished she had not escaped.

"He asked the governor to have the marshes searched all the way to Darien."

Christine sniffled. "It would take an army to search that far, and besides, they're gone now. They sailed away into the night."

Dolly studied her with damp eyes. "It's a miracle. That's what it is. To have endured such an ordeal and make it home all in one piece." She hesitated. "You are alright, aren't you? They didn't..."

Christine got her meaning and shook her head with force. "No, Dolly. I was well-treated, almost like a lady. I thought they meant to marry me off to a lonely planter in the Indies, but for some reason, they kept me aboard and carried me back home."

"Maybe they meant to bring you back."

Christine raised a shoulder as if she didn't know. "I did their mending and other chores."

Dolly scowled. "And Alligator George? Did you see him? Was he as horrible as they say?"

"Yes," spat Christine, surprised at her vehemence. The memory of being tossed into the wobbly little boat and sent off across the dark ocean stabbed her in the heart again. He'd tossed her overboard without so much as a goodbye or good luck. He'd abandoned her just like Elias had abandoned poor Anya.

"He was horrible, that Alligator George. Ugly and rude and very selfish." Saying it made Christine's eyes well up with tears, and she let them spill over. She missed the open sea. She missed the *Siren*, and worse of all, she missed Nathan. She hated herself for it.

Dolly gasped and threw herself back into Christine's lap. They laid that way until dinner and Christine begged her friend to stay.

CHAPTER THIRTEEN

Nathan tied off at the docks, evaded any probing questions, and decided to stick to his usual routine of waiting for cargo to be stowed away into the warehouse before he departed.

He'd slept little after the privateer's search and had to force himself to get up as the *Siren* trudged upriver. The tension aboard had diminished, and there was a feeling of false bravado that they'd gotten away with it.

Seven of his men, young and fierce and loyal, came to him as soon as they were dismissed and asked to be let go. They weren't interested in lesser pay and the boredom of an honest merchantman, and with a word of warning and a final oath to take the *Dragon's* secret to their graves, he agreed.

He took drink late into the night with Mr. Walker and a few friends at a tavern. He learned that Mr. Fryer's daughter had been rescued along a road that led from Savannah by a fisherman and his wife. Nathan then sent a message to Mathew outside of town. Passing over a few coins, he took his rest upstairs before heading to Clearwater in the morning.

The streets of Savannah bustled with wagons and carts at dawn, and further into town carriages stopped at shop windows showing off hats and shawls and pottery. The tobacco shop looked busy, and he waved at a few local gentlemen who nodded as he cantered by.

He could not race the old nag he'd rented home. He didn't want to raise suspicions, and he hoped the leisurely ride would allow Mathew time to make it to Clearwater so that they could tie up loose ends. He would also need to apologize.

His friend-turned-business associate might never forgive him for ruining his sister. Excuses rose in Nathan's mind as he traveled along. He avoided the marsh and took the old road back to Clearwater, making every effort to appreciate the pleasantly cool conditions of the morning. By the time he reached the old plantation, his mind was made up. He would apologize to Mathew, give him his cut of the revenue from the Indies trip, and assure him that he would take care of Christine and her reputation if necessary.

How people would talk, he knew; how society would judge her, especially other women. Mrs. Blakemore flitted through his mind. She would lift her nose and turn her back as quickly as anyone. The hypocrisy disgusted him.

Upon reaching his land, the first view of Clearwater lifted his spirits. The windows gleamed in the sunshine, and the front garden glowed with late roses. He felt the aching knot in-between his shoulders relax. Isaac would be here, anxious and eager to hear it all. He hoped there was better news of Christine.

After the horse was taken from his hands, his boots removed, and a pitcher of ale gulped down, Nathan strode into the study to examine his letters. There was nothing of urgent concern, so he collapsed into a well-bound chair and considered the empty fireplace. He wondered how long it was until autumn's blustery peak when he could sit by the fire and get lost in his thoughts. It wasn't that far away.

The sound of horse hooves made him get up, and he saw through the window that Mathew had arrived. Nathan watched him bound up the steps on the front of the house, but he waited for a servant to let his friend up. Riding boots echoed up the stairs, and Nathan waited at the door to greet him. Mathew nearly burst through the door frame when he saw him there. His face was lit with excited curiosity but also shadowed with concern.

"Mathew!" Nathan reached for his arm to shake it and dragged him into the room.

Mathew made a beeline for his favorite chair. "I've seen her," he panted, then caught himself and lowered his tone. "I went into town straight away when I heard from Papa. She's weak and tired and a little burned from the sun."

"Yes?" urged Nathan.

Mathew continued. "When I spoke with her, she insisted she heard a noise that night and thought she saw me leaving and went out alone."

"To the marsh?"

"No," Mathew shook his head. "The story is she saw something out her window and went outside thinking it might be me—then found herself out walking and was snatched in the dark."

"That much is true, but in Savannah?"

"Yes."

Nathan furrowed his brows. "She's changed the story a bit."

"It's better that way. She's made no mention of the marsh, which puts her far away from Clearwater and the inlet."

"It puts pirates in Savannah."

"Well, we know those scoundrels come and go through the tunnels," relented Mathew. "I told her I received a message, but she did not let on that she knew about it."

"She did know," said Nathan. "She was furious at the time, but I had no choice. And I suppose she's furious with me still."

"She hasn't said. She keeps to her room and stays quiet."

Nathan leaned back in his chair and pushed a carafe toward his friend. "We were chased," he said in a low tone, and Mathew looked over his shoulder as if someone was listening.

"It was the *Hornet*, but we used our disguise and let her chase us into the dark. When I came up just south of the inlet, I could not risk it, so we sent her off in a small pirogue within reach of the shoals."

"She did all that?" Mathew stroked his chin. "She claims she was dumped along one of the small inlets and walked for days."

Nathan smiled a little. "It was only a day's walk, maybe two. I appreciate her embellishments."

"It protects us all." Mathew frowned. "And the goods?"

"I could not unload them. I had to bring them into port. No one was the wiser, I hope. They're still aboard."

"No one's looking. They're all passing around rumors about my sister."

Nathan's stomach tightened. "How is old Hawthorne? I suppose he'll withdraw his attentions now that she's been had by pirates."

To his surprise, Mathew shook his head. "Papa called on him just hours after Christine's rescue. I thought it was all put to rest, but Papa is anxious to see her off, and as lucratively as possible."

"And have a chance to win the Hawthorne house," said Nathan in disgust, "when he's dead." Everyone coveted the fine Hawthorne house.

"Yes," agreed Mathew with a snarl. "Papa would be happy to move in with my widowed sister and take over her finances."

"Well, at least she's ruined now," said Nathan then realized he'd spoken aloud. "I mean, she's not," he said in a rush, forcing a laugh at his rude insinuation. "I only meant that she does not have to marry if she wishes although people might think..."

"Yes," said Mathew, his mouth dropping into a solemn line. "I don't know what she will do if Hawthorne writes her off for then surely everyone else will, too. But I don't think that she'd mind it." He glanced at Nathan and a spark of blame lit in his eye.

A spark lit in Nathan's heart, too, but for an entirely different reason. Before he could stop himself, he said, "No worries, my friend. This was my fault from the start, and I quite admire your little sister. I'll see she's treated well and her reputation restored." He glanced around his library, now illustrious and fine. "I'll marry her," he promised Mathew, and when his friend widened his eyes in surprise, Nathan leaned back and gave a careless shrug. "I'll court her and marry her before Christmas, and we'll have a ball at this fine place. Everything will be forgotten."

LATE SUMMER FLOWERS had nearly bloomed away, and the trees' arms hung low, laden down with a season's worth of foliage in their hands as their crowns began to color. It would not be many weeks before the leaves dried out and crumbled to the ground.

On Thursday, Papa had visitors in his study, and Christine crept out to the back courtyard and sat in the shade with a book on cookery she'd filched from the kitchen because she could not bear to open the family bible. Abigail brought her tea then puttered about the yard like she was too afraid to let her out of sight.

After Dolly's visit, Christine had determined to rise and dress the next morning and receive visitors in the parlor. To her mild surprise, they did not come. Abigail passed along two messages from different neighbors who had known her since she was a child, and Papa bade her good morning each day at breakfast before hurrying away to call on his associates. She read and sewed a little, but spent most of the day staring out the front window watching people walk or ride up and down the street.

Matty came to visit. He was now permanently moved away to oversee the construction of his new home and would soon be in want of a wife. He sat with Christine a bit and mentioned in passing that he had seen the *Siren* come in and visited with Captain Butler at Clearwater Plantation.

It seemed all the air in the parlor seeped out the windows when he mentioned Nathan, but she only stared like it didn't matter to her at all.

"He asked about you," Matty said when she didn't reply.

Christine glanced at the closed parlor door. "I hope he's well," she said at last.

He studied her, and she looked away so he could not see the melancholy in her heart. "He is healthy as an ox," said Matty. "Should I tell him hello from you next time we meet? Or maybe we should have him to dinner?"

"No." Christine's heart burned. "No, I..." She glanced at the door. "We can't have him here."

Matty leaned back on the settee and stretched out a leg. "Why not?" He lowered his voice. "There's no reason not to welcome him here. No one's the wiser. And you are feeling better, aren't you?"

Christine's heart lurched at the thought of seeing Nathan again. "He threw me overboard, Matty, and abandoned me on my own. Besides, this is Papa's house. He has no use for him."

"It wasn't straight into the sea, Christine," Matty chided her. "You were just a short paddle from shore, and see, you made it home safe and sound. Thanks to you, everything is alright, and we can all move forward from here."

"Legally, I hope."

"Yes," said Matty. "The laws have changed, times have changed, and we're going to adapt."

"Well, that's very good."

He stared at her, and it made her uncomfortable. "How did you find the Indies? I'm a bit envious, you know."

Memories of palm trees and dolphins and the waterfall came crashing back. The breathtaking happiness they had brought her made her smile. Christine looked down at her hands. "I liked it very much." She glanced sideways at him. "It was like a painting come to life that looked like heaven and tasted exotic and wonderful."

"Hot?"

She chuckled. "Oh, my, yes, but not if one knew where to huddle away from the midday sun." She sighed over her recollections. "The trees and flowers there are the most beautiful things."

"Yes, you always did like your flowers," mused Mathew.

"I brought some home that would have looked beautiful pressed, but... they're gone." Christine's heart became heavy again, and the happy reminiscing ended. It was all past, like a foggy dream.

"I'm sorry," said Matty in a low tone, "and I know Captain Butler is, too."

She felt the old familiar knot in her throat at the mention of his name.

"Perhaps you would be open to seeing him again and pretend as if nothing happened."

"Perhaps," she said, even though her heart cried out that she could not bear to meet him in passing and pretend they had never been familiar.

A rattle of horse and carriage out the window interrupted their quiet conversation. Matty leaped to his feet. "See now," he said with his usual enthusiasm, "one of your friends has come to call. I should get on."

He kissed her on her cheek and promised to return soon, and she braced herself not to tear up and plead for him to move back home. The house was a lonely place even with Abigail around. How could she explain that she missed her little closet aboard the *Siren*?

The sound of footfalls echoed in the hall as visitors came and went. She heard Papa's voice and understood he was home from his calls and would go into the study after telling Matty good day. She doubted Papa would check on her in the parlor that had become her prison. Walking out of doors was forbidden now—for everyone would stop and stare and wonder why she was risking it. Papa couldn't bear anymore scandal. How long did one wait to venture into society again after being kidnapped by pirates?

A knock on the parlor door jerked her from her reverie.

"Miss Christine?" Abigail had a brooding look on her face, and Christine wondered why she was still fretting over her.

"I'm fine, Abigail," she said, forcing a chuckle, "and hardly finished with my knitting."

"It's only I wanted to tell you that Mr. Hawthorne has come to call."

Christine froze; her mind became slippery, and she couldn't think.

"Shall I bring him in?" Abigail looked like she did not want to let him in, but they both knew what had to be done. Dash Papa and his meddling ways! Now he had brought their family friend here to shame them all.

Abigail was still staring, and Christine knew Hawthorne was not far away, probably just a few steps from the door listening as hard as he was able.

"Of course," she said in a clipped tone and rose from her chair. The knitting slid to the floor, but she left if there, stiffening her back when Mr. Hawthorne walked into the room holding his riding crop with both hands.

NATHAN RODE INTO TOWN to check his inventory at the warehouse. He'd quietly ordered extra molasses carried out to Clearwater where Isaac would drive it through villages and hamlets along the coast to sell.

Two of his men stood outside the warehouse looking grim when he approached, but they said nothing as he slipped inside. He should have recognized their hard stares as warnings, for when he entered, his manager stood in the middle of their lumber glaring at one of the officials from the docks.

The underhanded leader of the trio, Mr. Young, looked like a porcupine with wiry hair and a bulbous stomach hanging over the tops of his trousers. His olive-colored coat was frayed along the edges, and his yellow waistcoat smudged with dust and tar.

Nathan's feet kept moving although his mind cautioned him to stop and organize his thoughts. Young had once offered to work on the *Siren*, but he'd been rejected.

"There you are," said Mr. Young, whipping his head around at Nathan's approach. "I've called two days in a row and was about to ride out to Clearwater."

It was then that Nathan noticed two militiamen browsing through his goods with interest. "Is something wrong?"

"Wrong?" said Young in a flustered tone. "You have a warehouse full of sugar, molasses, and rum, and I have an agent who says your numbers don't add up."

"You're doing my mathematics?" Nathan tried to sound confident enough to tease him, but Young grew red around the mouth.

"I know when a ship sits low in the water, and yours does not. For such a successful merchant, Captain Butler, your ship leaves half-full and returns just as light. I'm amazed at your good fortune."

"We don't weigh down so much that she can't catch the wind," reproved Nathan. "There are dangers at sea, Young," he reminded him, "and I like to have the weather gauge and a fast ship should I run into foul weather—or characters." The hint of pirates and privateers shut the man up for a few beats but not long enough.

"Still," whined Young, "I am not satisfied you have amassed such a fortune by shipping out a few loads of lumber and rice a few times a season."

Nathan bit his tongue so he did not tell the man it was none of his business. Clearly, Young had overheard tales of Clearwater's restoration and that Captain Butler had deep pockets.

"Your father lost everything as I understood it," said Young, "yet you have the finest house in Savannah."

Nathan looked him dead in the eye. "The Butlers have always been a family of fortune, Mr. Young," he retorted, "and I cannot help that my loyalty to the rebellion left my home in disrepair. And as you know, Clearwater does not sit in Savannah, but I thank you for the compliment, although I must disagree. Mr. Hawthorne has more than one fine house and a great estate, too. I'm humbled to be counted among his company."

Young snorted. There was a gleam of perspiration across his forehead, and Nathan realized he was nervous.

"You have never liked me, Young, I know," he said. "I'm sorry I would not take you on when I started my business, but you did not strike me as a sailor and see how well you are better suited for the docks."

The would-be purser glared. "I know I would have done far better managing your accounts than you have done." He clenched a handful of rolled papers in his fist. "I have an inventory of your goods these past six months, and your cargo this week far exceeds what you have brought in before."

"I felt like taking a risk," said Nathan.

The man stared. "I want to see all of your books," he insisted. "If your cargo on the ledgers matches the inventory you have in your warehouse we will have no problems."

Nathan locked his jaw to keep from growling.

Mr. Young motioned toward two militiamen watching their tense exchange. "And these gentlemen," he said with a sly grin, "will escort you to the jail for questioning."

"Jail? To what end?" It was all Nathan could do not to shout. His warehouse manager paled, but he waved him off.

"We have questions for you, Captain Butler," said Young, now more confident. "A Miss Christine Fryer was abducted the day after your last departure, and she has just been returned as you've come home."

"And so?" Nathan dared him to make an accusation.

"The *Hornet* reports you were sighted in the same waters as *The Dragon*. Perhaps you know something about Alligator George that you could share with us."

"I know nothing," Nathan insisted.

"Well, then you have nothing to worry about. Whoever is aiding pirates along the coast will be caught eventually."

He motioned for the guards to escort him out, and Nathan gave them a polite bow. "Let me collect a few things," he told them. With heart pounding, he slunk into the office to grab his altered ledgers and jot down instructions for his manager, then, forcing a confident sneer on his face, he strode out and accompanied the militia the several blocks to the jail.

CHRISTINE CAME TO HER feet and waited for Hawthorne to greet her. The parlor door had been latched behind him, and Papa's voice faded away. The house fell silent as a tomb. All she could hear was her heart oozing along. She'd hoped Hawthorne would not come to call and that their brief acquaintanceship would be forgotten.

"Miss Fryer," he said in his kind but raspy voice, "I hope you are well."

She lowered her gaze to the floor.

"I inquired of your Papa as soon as you were found and sent my well wishes. I do hope he passed them along to you."

Christine dipped her chin to acknowledge it as her cheeks warmed. The man walked across the room and stood in front of the window blocking her view should she want to look up and outside.

"What a dreadful circumstances you have endured. I'm happy to see you are safe now. Your father says you are quite recovered and that despite the experience, you were treated well."

She forced herself to meet his eyes. "Well enough," she assured him.

He smiled with fondness. "I'm happy to hear it."

Christine blinked and looked away, and after a moment's silence, he cleared his throat. "I understand it will come to no surprise to you that your Papa and I have discussed a union between yourself and me."

The air in Christine's lungs was snatched by some unseen force. She could not move. She didn't expect Mr. Hawthorne to bring up so sensitive a subject—not today. Her knees gave way, and she sank back down into her seat. She opened her mouth, but nothing came out. Heat rose up her neck and into her cheeks, and nausea sank her stomach like a stone.

"Now, now," he chided, sensing her distress. He waved a hand in the air as if shooing away a floating dandelion seed. "I do not mean to cause you any discomfort. I only hoped to re-assure you that I have nothing but admiration and respect for you—and your fine home and family. I would be honored to be your husband," he said and then bowed his head.

Christine thought she would be sick. He was not asking for her hand in marriage but telling her he would kindly do her a favor. "I thank you, Mr. Hawthorne," she stuttered when she could think of nothing else to say.

"Say the word, and it is done," he assured her.

She felt horrified. She could not say the word. He had not even dropped to his knees. But she was glad of it. She tried to be brave and meet his gaze. He smiled again, but it was laced with pity. The worst kind of admiration.

Before she could think of how to extricate herself from this painful and humiliating situation, he bent over with a qui-et groan and dropped down to one unsteady leg. Christine thought she would faint.

"My dear Miss Fryer," Hawthorne said in a strained but congenial voice, "would you do me the honor of being my bride?"

Heat showered across her shoulders as Christine wavered in her chair. It was so hot, her palms felt like they were drip-ping. Her pulse throbbed in her ears. She chanced a look into Hawthorne's watery eyes and saw that he was staring with pa-tience and expectation.

"I'm... I..." Where was Matty — no — Nathan Butler when she needed him? Christine's mind swirled for the right words. Papa would disown her if she refused. "I.. May I think on it?" she asked, nearly gasping for air. It was the first step in refusing a gentleman and left the door open to send a refusal through a messenger.

"Of course, my dear," said Mr. Hawthorne. He hauled himself to his feet and dusted off his trousers as if her floors were dirty then he picked up his hat from the table where he'd placed it before the performance. It was all an act, she realized, a routine expected by their society.

He considered her from across the room. "I didn't mean to surprise you, but I wanted you to know that I understand you and pity your circumstances." He dipped his chin in a show of humility. "I am a mature man, Miss Fryer, and I don't make judgments on the misfortunes of others. Whatever happened to you in the Indies and aboard that dreadful ship of scallywags, why, I would never hold those things against you."

Too shocked to respond, Christine moved her gaze to the floor and stared at nothing.

"I'll wish you good afternoon then," he said and backed toward the door.

She collected herself, rose to her feet, and curtsied. "Thank you, Mr. Hawthorne," she said in a hoarse voice. She was thankful that it did not crack.

He shut the door, and Christine collapsed into the chair again with a hand to her heart. She wished she could slow it down or smother it out. Perspiration coated her skin, and she realized her shift was damp and her neck soaking.

The old man had finally done it—cowed to Papa's encouragement and perhaps even a bribe. A simple marriage arrangement would give Hawthorne a young companion to care for him in his final years, and she would bring a fine dowry as well.

Christine swallowed a sour surge of bile down in her throat. Papa would be rid of his youngest child and her expenses. Perhaps he would marry again, too, although he was never one who sought the fussings of a woman.

The room began to float in small circles around her, and Christine closed her eyes to ward off the woozy dizziness. What was in it for her? Nothing. Nothing at all.

She retired to bed early and ignored the voices in the house the next morning. She did not want to see Papa, and she did not want to visit with Mr. Hawthorne or anyone else again.

Abigail brought her breakfast in bed, but she did not bother to eat it. She was growing thinner. Soon she would be properly fair again, but she doubted she would ever have the same complexion.

Heavy footfalls down the hall filled her with dread, and Christine turned her back to the door. Let Papa think she was sleeping, or better, ill. Too ill to marry his old friend and business partner.

There came a brief knock, but the door opened before she could respond. It was shut with a brisk click, and she looked over her shoulder, surprised to see Matty out of breath in his riding coat.

"Christine," he said in a low hiss.

She noted his dusty boots. His hair was wild and wind-blown. She sat up with disquiet. "What is it?"

Matty glanced over his shoulder at the closed door then back. "It's Butler."

Her heart heaved in her chest. She'd been trying to forget Nathan Butler, to forget about everything, not just the Indies, but her feelings wouldn't go away. And there were so many.

"What has he done now?" She swung her legs over the sides of the bed. "Is he hurt?"

Matty shook his head. "Worse. He's been taken to the jail for an interview."

Her mind swam with confusion. "Because of me?"

He walked over and dropped beside her. In an even quieter tone, he whispered, "One of the officials for the port, that Mr. Young, asked to see the ledgers and the warehouse. Word has spread around the *Hornet* came upon them at dawn after a midnight pirate chase."

The room began to spin. Christine felt like she was falling over.

"We have to do something," said Matty, and he pounded his fist into his hand. "Not just for us, for him. He's my... well, he's been my very good friend this many years and through the war although I did not bring him around. Papa, you know."

"Yes," mumbled Christine. The Butlers weren't good enough company with their madness and poverty.

"Their plantation failed, the war came, his father's wife died—my heart—it would drive any man mad."

"He was true to the end, though," said Christine. "Mr. Butler was loyal to the cause and stood up to the British with his very last breath. That's why he tried to burn down his house. It wasn't quite lunacy, he didn't want them to have it."

"He had Quaker roots and was an abolitionist. He understood what true independence meant."

"He died of a broken heart, I suppose," said Christine. "But Nathan, he can't be caught! They'll hang or shoot him." She suddenly forgave him everything—even throwing her overboard like poor Anya.

"It's that vengeful weasel of a man," said Matty in a furious tone. "Mr. Young offered to serve as pursuer on the *Siren* but was refused."

"We have to do something but what?"

"I thought I would ride in and speak for him."

"You'd be suggesting that you're involved."

"There has to be a way. I can alter my own ledgers again. Papa knows there're inconsistencies. I'll claim the extra inventory at the warehouse, and say that it's mine. I'll pay on it—tariffs and all."

"But your home and land."

"I have enough, and Butler would pay me back over time."

Christine's mind swam, trying to collect her bobbing concerns. "What about the *Hornet*? They've raised suspicions now."

"Well, they can't accuse him of piracy if you share your account of your abduction."

She furrowed her brows. "You mean tell my story to the authorities?"

Matty nodded. "You must describe what you heard and saw with the 'pirates.' Make sure there is no way the *Siren* could have been involved."

"I would have to lie." Christine put a hand to her throat. How far would she go to save a man she... loved. Oh dear. She'd fallen for a smuggler. It was true. There was no use denying it. Saving him was more important than her silly reputation.

"He's no pirate. It wouldn't really be a lie," suggested Matty.

"If I say that I never saw Nathan—I mean, Captain Butler—or heard mention of his ship they'd have to believe him."

"Especially since you escaped. Tell them the pirates came about because they had no contacts in the north. Say they returned to the Florida coast where they meant to stay because they didn't want trouble with anyone from Savannah."

"That just might work," said Christine, twisting the coverlet in her hands, "I could say they realized kidnapping me was a mistake. But I'm dreadful at a fib, Matty."

"You must do it, and in many ways, it's not a lie, just a story. You know Butler and his crew aren't pirates, so it's a tale to protect them. In that way, it makes it true."

"Honorable, at least?"

He put an arm around her shoulders. "You will always be honorable to me."

Christine took a deep breath and slid to her feet. "Let me dress and call for the carriage, and we'll go at once." A bump at the door made her stop.

It creaked open, and Papa stood there with wide eyes and red cheeks. "What is this?" he asked in a low, irritated tone. "Mathew, why is your sister up and all distraught? You know she must rest." He gave Christine a piercing stare. "Mr. Hawthorne is awaiting your reply."

Christine glanced at Matty telling him everything with one look. He seemed to understand at once.

"Papa," he said, but the man held out a hand to hush him. "I asked you not to interfere in your sister's arrangement," he said in an angry tone.

"But she doesn't love him, and he's more than twice her age!"

"Enough!"

The shout echoed off the ceiling and almost shook Christine's resolve. She dashed across the room to fetch her dressing gown. "I cannot marry Mr. Hawthorne, Papa," she cried, cringing as she waited for him to roar.

"Captain Butler is in danger," said Matty, standing between them. "They think he's in business with Alligator George. I've asked Christine to accompany me to speak on his behalf. She knows he's not a pirate."

"Butler? Pirate? She will not go," retorted Papa.

Christine watched his face turn scarlet, shuddering as she covered herself and waited for them to leave so she could change.

"He'll be convicted." Matty's voice trembled.

"The Butler family is not our concern," Papa stormed back, "but the reputation of Christine and this dreadful situation is. We are lucky that even Hawthorne will have her now."

Matty let out an exasperated breath. "He's an old man, Papa, and Christine's adventure will be forgotten with time. Let her marry whom she chooses. She takes the dowry no matter what."

"She's had her chance, and she chose no one."

Papa's falsehood shot through Christine's heart like a flaming arrow. She raised her shoulders and glared. "I never had the opportunity to choose," she retorted. "The Talbots were not wealthy enough. Every suitor who showed any interest was too young or too poor or not high enough to suit you."

"We are Fryers," said Papa in a staccato burst. "I will not have you end up, like, well like the Butler family."

"I admire the Butler family," snapped Christine. She rather enjoyed the look of shock on Papa's face at the moment, but it did not last. She braced herself. "I will go with Matty, Papa, and I will defend Captain Butler. He is no pirate. I should know, shouldn't I?"

She let him absorb the shock of her words, but it didn't take him long to recover. He pointed at her with a finger as sharp as a sword. "You will not go, I forbid it."

"Let her go. She knows what's best for her, even if you don't care," interrupted Matty. He backed away a few steps as he said it, and Christine feared Papa would strike him. He turned purple and sweat glimmered at his temples. He was so stunned he could not catch enough breath to bellow into the rafters.

"Get dressed now, Christine," Matty commanded. "We will speak for Captain Butler and then I will take you to Dolly's to spend a day or two." He faced her but spoke loudly enough so their father could hear. "You may send your refusal to Mr. Hawthorne from there." He stomped out of the room and down the stairs.

Christine gathered her courage to peek at her papa and found him still there. His eyes were as large as dinner plates and his cheeks on fire. He glowered like he might raise his hand to her if she dared to leave.

"You will not go," he said in a horrid, cutting tone, "if I have to lock you in your room until the wedding. I won't allow you to ruin yourself for all of Savannah to see. Either you marry

Hawthorne, or I will cut you off. I'll cut you both off!" he roared, and it echoed through the house.

Christine's arms and legs shook, and she sank to the floor. Her bedroom door slammed as he left, cracking the boards around the hinges. When she was sure he was downstairs, she tried to collect herself. Her heart galloped like a runaway horse as tears streamed down her face. There was more than one jail in Savannah.

CHAPTER FOURTEEN

In the old colony jail, Nathan was locked inside a small storage room. The boards of the structure seemed to bake in the warm sun. He walked over to a small window and looked out across the dry and empty street. Treetops swished like silk gowns. Their leaves were beginning to change color. He wondered if Christine had left her house; if she had slipped back into the marsh to observe the beginnings of a new season. Did she miss seeing him like he missed her?

Upon arriving, a government official had questioned Nathan mercilessly. He had, what Nathan suspected, a report from the *Hornet* and perhaps written accusations from Mr. Young. The port's authorities had been paying closer attention to the *Siren's* arrivals and departures than he thought.

He'd shown them his ledgers, his route, the weather reports, and all of his conveniently smudged inventory books. Mr. Walker and the other *Siren* officers had feigned complete and total ignorance, and that had saved them for now, but the fear of piracy had stirred up a heated excitement around the city and now everyone was eyeing Nathan—mad Mr. Butler's heir—with suspicion.

He was brought no food or water. Late in the day when a man unlocked the door, Nathan looked up hoping at least for a bit of day-old bread. It was the militia escort again.

"They would like to see you," one said in a polite tone, and Nathan nodded. His meager confidence waned when he saw they held wrist irons. He swallowed. Luck had taken a turn for the worse.

Led away to be questioned once more, he held his head high. They had no proof, he told himself, only conjecture, unless one of the crew talked. Two heavy doors were pushed open, and Nathan was taken to a chair that sat across from his own personal jury—an inquiry board of officers and authorities, including a lawyer, with pensive looks on their faces. "A few more questions," said the official in charge, and Nathan mashed his lips together to keep from protesting.

He dropped into the chair with his stomach grumbling. The other men had had time for a meal and probably a rest, but they did not mean to let him lie his tired head down long enough to come up with more stories. A few chairs scuffled behind him, and he realized there were spectators. Mr. Young leered at him from the first row.

The proceeding began again with a shuffle of papers. "We have now a report," said the superior, "that you are oft-seen coming up along the shoreline and sometimes in and out of the hammocks and cays."

Nathan raised a shoulder. "Maybe once or twice," he admitted. "My property is south of Savannah, as you know, and I have been known to stop along the way to let off a drunken hand and send him ashore."

"And you've never seen pirates? "

He tried to look confused. "I have seen ships I did not recognize. They're in the books. We never give chase, we're merchants, not privateers. I'm only interested in my own business."

"And your business brought you to Savannah along the same course as the *Dragon* this week past."

He pressed his lips together, thinking. "If there was a *Dragon* in the area, I did not see her," he insisted. "Perhaps she came up close along the coast in the dark. We did not."

"And the inconsistencies with your cargo?"

"I've explained that the best I can," said Nathan, trying to sound annoyed. "I'm sorry I am a poor bookkeeper. I am new to shipping. I was a planter's son. I will do better and hire one."

"You will be fined at the very least," said a captain in a serious tone.

Nathan tried to look disappointed and embarrassed.

Another authority spoke up, eyeing Mr. Young, and Nathan knew Young had the man in his pocket. "I am not satisfied with your excuses, sir. Every report of the *Dragon* in Savannah coincides with your leave."

"There are many ships going in and out of the river at all times," replied Nathan. "I'm sure many vessels share the same coincidence." He felt his forehead dampen and cursed the telltale sign. They were getting to him, making him literally sweat. He had no patron to protect him; no respected family reputation to excuse him. Bored and eager men out to make a name for themselves in the southern Republic would come after him.

"Tell us the hideaway of Alligator George," said the captain in a surprising turn, "and we will capture him, and he can exonerate you."

"But I don't know it," said Nathan. He furrowed his brow. The captain had become the accuser now; he'd only pretended to be friendly to relax him.

A wobbly-chinned man from the port spoke again. "We know you are involved in something illicit," he insisted. "Mr. Young and the records speak for themselves, as does your own schedule."

"It's coincidence," Nathan insisted, nearly rising to his feet. He cast a hateful look over his shoulder at Young who smiled back with glee. "Mr. Young," he said, returning his gaze to the table of inquisitors, "is a poor sailor and a vengeful man. I regret I did not hire him when he applied for a position on the *Siren* five years ago; I did not know he would trouble himself to seek a petty sort of revenge."

The jury stared as if Nathan was making it all up, and he took a deep breath in frustration. "Interview my men if you like."

"We have," said the captain sternly, "and they've all stuck to their stories—the ones we can find. Everyone claims to have never met Alligator George at sea. Where is your crew, Captain Butler?"

"On leave," he replied, "but I have let some go."

"And why is that?"

"Because," replied Nathan, suddenly knowing what to say, "I do not pay enough to suit them. Does that sound like I'm up to no good in our waters, good sirs?"

The men studied him, and someone in the room cleared his throat. Behind him, Young stood up. "If I may," he said in a sneering voice, "perhaps Captain Butler is actually Alligator George himself, and the missing crew members want nothing more to do with a pirate that kidnaps young maidens. They've escaped his service to find legitimate employment."

The men at the table looked around at one another and some seemed to consider this new theory. "Your ship will be searched, Captain Butler," said the captain, "from bow to stern. And your warehouse, too. If we find a connection to Alligator George of any kind, you will be tried and could be hung as a pirate. Do you understand?"

Nathan's throat constricted, but he did not allow himself to swallow lest they notice. It'd be better to admit that he engaged in a little smuggling, but it would ruin everyone involved. He couldn't do that to Mathew. He wouldn't do it to Christine. He loved the girl. Instead, he squared his shoulders and remained silent.

"Take him back to his room," said the captain to the guard. He turned back to Nathan. "There you will be detained until you find a way to clear your name."

Nathan's soul wilted. There was no way he could clear himself locked up in a storage room, and they knew it. Young had somehow convinced them that he knew something of the *Dragon* and was most likely involved in the occasional piracy off-shore.

His throat went dry at his bleak chances. The revolution was over. He had no one on his side. Soon there would be a judge and an executioner.

The door burst open and a messenger flew past him to the table. He watched and hoped that it was good news, but it was not meant for him. The guard clapped the irons back around his wrists, and he was led back to his quarters—by bayonet tip this time.

NATHAN SUFFERED IN the stuffy, damp small room by day and shivered when temperatures dropped that night. His dreams were haunted by his father's face. Sometimes, they'd brighten for a moment, and he'd see himself at the rail beside Christine studying her profile. It was the only thing that kept him calm.

At sunrise, he sat itching on the edge of his nit-infested cot. He wasn't sure what day it was or how long it'd been since they'd arrested him at the warehouse. A guard brought a pitcher of briny water with a stone-faced expression and handed him a bruised apple. He ate it in three bites.

Hammering sounds echoed in the distance, and his imagination ran wild, wondering if they were building a scaffold to hang him. So soon? He'd hardly been allowed to defend himself and had not been offered any help in his defense. They were treating the issue as a naval matter which meant little fairness and a speedy result. He might never even see a real judge.

That was what Young wanted anyway. It was almost unbelievable. He was accused of being in business with or being the actual apparition of Alligator George himself—an imaginary buccaneer he'd brought to life and now would die for.

Nathan ran his fingers through his unkempt hair. His jaw felt prickly, with two days of stubble. They'd impounded his ship and questioned him like a criminal. Well, what else did he expect? They hadn't even mentioned his service during the war. He'd fought for this country. He harmed no one with his comings and goings in the marsh. The smuggling had been a small thing until the tariffs had been set down in '89, and then the story of the *Dragon* had grown beyond his control. It'd amused him so much that he'd let it. Now he might hang for it.

The clapping of boots on the ground made him stand and peek through the window. They were coming for him. And so early, too. His stomach sank. Surely, they had better things to do. He had the right to more time and a defense.

Nathan held out his hands when they opened the door and ignored the bayonets pointing his direction. Tired, he let them drag him back to the hall to be questioned yet again. His mind was in a fog, he realized, and if he wasn't exact in his answers and matched them perfectly to what he'd said before, they would cross him up. His knees threatened to buckle. He let out a tired breath. It was happening so fast. He hadn't had time to prepare.

The doors were thrown open, and he was pushed inside. The board of men wore the same faces, and they did not look any happier. He was escorted to his chair and shoved down. With a thumping heart, he waited and prayed there would be nothing new. He was too exhausted to think clearly now.

"Bring them in," said the captain, and Nathan closed his eyes. The crew. He could not even look. They'd found the crew and now they would be forced to accuse him to save themselves. The full truth—smuggling—would not excuse them, but perhaps it would save their lives.

He waited with bated breath, staring at the whitewashed wall behind the heads of his examiners.

"State your name," said the captain in a loud, official tone.

"Miss Christine Fryer," came the calm, brave voice of a woman.

Nathan's heart leaped to the ceiling. He twisted her direction and looked—beautiful Christine. She was dressed smartly in a coffee-colored riding jacket with sparkling brass buttons.

Her shining hair was coiled up underneath her bergère. Fine leather riding boots made her look tall and queenly. The apples of her cheeks were splotched with color, and her bright silvery eyes glowed.

She did not meet his gaze. Behind her, Mathew stood with a hat in his hand. He gave Nathan a confident blink then looked away. The men at the table made some attempt to be gentle, but the questions became blunt.

She held her own: "Yes, I recognize this man. I have seen him in polite society among most of you." Some of Nathan's judges looked sheepish.

"No," she insisted, "he was not aboard the pirate ship. He is not Alligator George and certainly not one of that sort."

Another inquiry shot out. She couldn't recall what Alligator George looked like. And then, "It was a pirate ship, but I never saw action while I was held. What other ships I did see were not American."

After inquiring as to her health and recovery, the men quickly let her go. She was convincing, speaking truths, bent truths, but believing them. Nathan tried to reign in his hope that they would believe a woman.

"Thank you, Miss Fryer," said the captain, "and may I congratulate you on your engagement to Mr. Hawthorne. He is an especial friend of mine."

Nathan's heart exploded in his chest. He felt burning, withering pieces of it flutter to the soles of his feet. So, this was the cost. Her engagement would prove she had no romantic interest in him that would spurn her to testify.

Christine curtsied and turned to her brother. As she did so, her gaze swept over Nathan for a fleeting moment, but he saw nothing except determination. She was a fierce thing when fighting for those she loved, he recalled. But wait. What could that mean? Did she love him? Or was she really engaged to the old man? Mathew extended his arm toward her, and they walked confidently from the room. It fell quiet.

"Three of your business associates have written letters in your defense," said the captain from the table. "Your first officer has made a statement that matches your own." He glanced down at the papers in front of him and reshuffled them. "Along with Miss Fryer's account, we have no choice but to release you at this time."

Nathan managed to stand for their decision, but his knees nearly wavered and did him in. "Your books," the captain admonished, "will be reviewed in six months' time." He raised a serious brow. "I earnestly advise you to find a more proficient bookkeeper and to hire a purser."

"Yes, sir," said Nathan, and he made a slight bow to hide his trembling innards. Had he just escaped death? First from the bloody fingers of the Revolution and now this? He swore he would never smuggle so much as a hairpin ever again. The Butler legacy was over.

The guards stood aside and let him walk out on his own free accord. He made his way outside, squinting in the sunshine for Christine and Mathew, but they had already departed for their home in their elegant ward.

His pulse throbbed through his body, shaking his frame, as he walked through the narrow streets of Savannah. He should have set out immediately for home, but there was Mathew, he told himself, that he must thank. In his heart, he knew it was an excuse to see Christine again.

He'd nearly burst with adoration for her when he first saw her in the jail. In that moment, it didn't matter if he lived or died. All that counted was that she was safe and looking more than well. She'd radiated the Fryer authority.

But this Hawthorne matter. Was it real? He'd seen the dull look in her eyes when her engagement was mentioned. Her father must have forced her into it using the shame of her kidnapping. Perhaps he thought there was no one good for her now, but Nathan Butler would suit. He realized he cherished the idea of her as a lifelong companion. His entire being ached at the thought of losing her.

He strode through the small city he'd known all his days, inhaling the swirl of early autumn breezes that carried the scents of withering leaves, apples, and squashes from the market. They mingled with the tang of the sea air and the heady scent of graybeard—the Spanish moss.

Nathan let out a long, satisfied breath and looked down. He looked haggard, he realized, and it brought him to a halt. He studied himself in a window. His hair was disheveled, his face grizzled, and his clothes wrinkled and stale.

No. Clearwater plantation or not, he did not come close to what Hawthorne had to offer. Perhaps that's why she'd accepted him. Nathan Butler would always be a poor plantation boy in her eyes and a smuggler to boot. Mathew had brought her to the jail. She had probably rescued him out of pity.

Heart burning with frustration and despair, Nathan changed direction and hurried for the taverns along the river. He needed a drink and a horse to make his way home. It was time to forget about Christine Fryer.

CHAPTER FIFTEEN

Mr. Hawthorne called in the temperate autumn after-noon to take Christine on a promenade around the ward. Papa had insisted she wear her new gown despite the fact it was only a walk. She found the French style a bit shocking with the bodice tucked just under the bosom. The clinging layers swirled all around her knees. They were sure to stick to her when she walked, but Papa and Abigail fawned over her so much she was sure by year's end she'd be walking about in her shift to set the fashion standard for Savannah.

He arrived promptly, and Christine paced herself as she walked through the parlor to the front door where she let him help her with a lavender shawl. She tied her hat in a jaunty bow at her chin as her numb mind ticked off each step she must take to finish the morning stroll with the feeble man beside her. Within an hour, she could be back in her room and out of her tight shoes. She felt like a mill moving lifelessly in circles—propelled by an energy that was not her own—spinning around and around and going nowhere.

Papa had forced her hand. She'd steeled herself and followed him down to his study, where she promised she would marry Hawthorne if she was allowed to defend Captain Butler. Seeing her resolve and his wishes within reach, Papa had agreed.

He'd warned her he would see she went through with it. She would marry Mr. Hawthorne or be sent far away to live with her second cousin in Pennsylvania. She did not abhor the idea of being a lady's companion, but she could not bear the thought of leaving Matty and the seashore she so loved. Far away, Captain Butler would never ever be anything more than a dream.

Hawthorne led her down the steps into the sunshine, and a neighbor coming the other way stopped and curtsied low while she raved over Hawthorne's fine topper. Her eyes passed over Christine, but she managed a faint smile and *how-do-you-do* as Christine thanked her in a crisp tone.

Some of Savannah might stand aside from the tragic Miss Fryer, like she was a broken vase, but soon they would follow Hawthorne's lead. Christine understood well enough how connections and money mended the opinions of the fickle-minded.

They walked across the street into the park, and Hawthorne pointed out a young oak sapling that had survived the hot summer then asked about the new fashions coming out of England with France in turmoil.

It seemed Christine's mind went one way and her mouth another. It felt like her outsides were turning to wax as her heart melted away a little day by day. Something deep in her soul was fading away into a dark, cold pool.

Another couple, newly married from Charleston, stopped Mr. Hawthorne to congratulate him on his impending nuptials. Hawthorne admired the woman's little pug, and Christine tried to smile at it, too, although she found it spoiled and ugly. She missed the flaming red and green birds on St. William and wished she had brought one home. It made her chest hurt, so she tried not to breathe too heavily.

Hawthorne took her elbow and guided her past a small stone monument that was beginning to crumble. The observation made her waxy exterior crumble away, too, as tears pricked her eyes.

"Are you well?" asked Hawthorne.

She could not look at him. She would burst into tears.

"Miss Fryer?"

Christine gave a jerk of her head in some semblance of a nod. Hawthorne fell silent and dawdled beside her, waiting for her to finish her imitation of admiring the monument. "Oh," he said after a time and with a tinge of mild impatience in his voice, "there is Mr. Blakemore in his new carriage."

She looked, and he began to pull her across the park to meet him. Mrs. Blakemore was in the carriage, too. The horses were brought to a halt, and the two men greeted one another. Christine looked dully up at Mrs. Blakemore. She looked elegant in a fresh striped silk that was too fine for a morning ride, but the splendid clothes did not appeal to Christine nor did the woman. Mrs. Blakemore was much younger than her husband but older than Christine. The deriding glance the married lady gave her made Christine think she looked aged and ill-used.

The carriage passed, and Christine bowed her head when she realized Mr. Blakemore had said her name. Perhaps he said goodbye. Her ears heard nothing but sluggish sounds that dragged through her ears.

Hawthorne took her arm again, this time sliding his dry hand down to grasp her fingertips. She was glad she'd worn gloves and concentrated on not tripping over the cobblestones as they crossed over to the neighbors' row of fine houses that encased the square.

A gentleman stood across the street, just paces away, idling on the sidewalk. Her downcast eyes followed the buckled shoes and stockings up to a pair of dark breeches and then the hem of a sapphire blue coat. Christine's heart flew into her throat. She stopped, frozen in the middle of the street, her hand slipping from Hawthorne's grasp.

Captain Butler—Nathan—gazed back. When their eyes met, it seemed like everything around them became a fuzzy blur. All she could see was him. A fine white cravat was draped around his thick neck and layered neatly under his chin. A crisp black and new-looking cocked hat hung from his hand. He was an image to behold, and her breath caught in her lungs.

From somewhere far away, someone next to her repeated something, and a part of her mind reminded her that it was her name. She stared straight ahead.

The look on Nathan's face said something, too. His jaw was drawn and serious, but there was a softness in his piercing blue eyes that warmed her soul. He moved across the cobblestone street in four great strides, and she watched him come like he was a ghost.

"Miss Fryer!" It was Hawthorne. His croaky voice pricked her ear, but she could not move. She watched Nathan approach, afraid to speak, afraid to breathe...

"Miss Fryer," said Nathan, and his teasing tone sent a flurry of hot snowflakes across her shoulders. Her fingers tingled. Her heart began to beat again with renewed life. "How are you this fine autumn day?"

She gazed into his eyes which seemed to say so much more than hello. She felt pressure on her elbow from Hawthorne's hand and wondered if she would split in two.

Nathan glanced over at him. "Mr. Hawthorne. I did not see you there, but see, we are in the street." He offered his arm to Christine, and she felt him pull her from Hawthorne's grasp and did not care. Nathan squeezed her hand as she stumbled mutely to the side of the cobbled road. Oh, what must he think? She was taken now.

She swallowed, her heart slowing back down to a sick, rhythmic beat. She could never tell him that she'd fallen in love with him; how she felt the first moment she spied him in the marsh, how she'd fought puzzling feelings of admiration, or how she'd been disappointed at her discovery of his pursuits and then understanding and hopeful. Last and still, how she'd completely forgiven him and was full of burning feelings she knew to be passion. She felt her cheeks warm as he studied her then she realized Hawthorne stood behind him, staring at them both with wide-eyed shock.

Sensing her unease, Nathan looked over his shoulder. "Mr. Hawthorne. May I have a word with Miss Fryer? I'm afraid we have... unfinished business." He gave the man a curt nod before he could answer and turned back to her.

Christine's legs trembled. She peeked and saw Hawthorne frown and step back a few feet to stir his cane around in-between the cobblestones.

"Elias was a fool."

He'd lost her. Christine stared at Nathan in confusion. The corner of his mouth twitched. "Elias," he repeated, "Anya's fisherman. Don't you remember? He let them throw her over-board."

Christine's heart tingled. Anya's pool. A pool of tears—tears as blue as Nathan's eyes. She'd certainly cried enough of her own to fill a pond these past weeks.

Nathan squeezed her hand. "I have no intention, Christine, of letting the sea or the maneuverings of men stop me from keeping you by my side."

She felt her mouth drop slightly in surprise even as her chest burned with pleasure at his bold words.

"Are you really engaged?"

Christine tried to bend her neck and nod, but tears welled up in her eyes in answer. Hawthorne smacked his cane on the ground and dove between them with a burst of a young man's energy. "She is," he said in a stern tone. "She accepted me weeks ago, and we are soon to be wed." He gave Nathan a disapproving stare.

Nathan turned on him like a provoked dog, and Christine saw the man she'd seen angry in the marsh, fierce on deck, and proud in the ballrooms of Savannah.

"She has no doubt been forced into the arrangement, Hawthorne. Her fortune is a great temptation, I am sure, but if you cared for her at all, you'd see that she made her own choice."

The man sputtered. "To who? You? A planter's son? A mad and sinful lunatic who took a—"

Before he could insult his stepmother, Nathan threw himself forward into Hawthorne, his chest nearly knocking him over. "Watch yourself. I'm half your age and twice the shot. You don't want to duel with me unless you need a ticket to an early grave."

Hawthorne paled. "Why you—"

"Pirate?"

Christine gasped. Couples strolling across the ward's park stopped to stare. After an eternal pause, Hawthorne stepped back. He dusted off his coat and glanced at Christine.

"If you intend to stand in the streets and engage in such a personal and private conversation with Captain Butler, Miss Fryer, I have no other choice but to see myself home." His cheeks were inflamed, and she felt sorry for him, but she reached inside of herself for a morsel of courage—an audacity that would ruin her and cut her off from her father, probably forever.

"You should leave, Mr. Hawthorne. Go on home. I'm sorry I cannot keep my word. I cannot..."

"She cannot marry you," finished Nathan.

Hawthorne blinked and humiliation turned to anger. "Of course she cannot," he said and spun around on his heel. It was almost as if he was relieved.

Christine watched the scene in muted horror. Nathan turned back to her, his face flushed. "And you won't, will you?"

"Well, I certainly can't now," she said in a strangled voice. She didn't know whether to laugh or to cry.

"Then it's as I hoped," he returned in a quiet voice. She gazed up at him. A sunbeam lit the top of his head up in a pool of light. He looked like a dark angel.

"And what will I do now," she said, breathless with concern yet swirling with anticipation.

He reached out and touched her chin. "Ride with me to the marsh. It's a lovely day." He waited with an anxious look for her reply. She glanced over her shoulder. "All alone?"

"You've been alone with me before."

She drew in a breath and answered, "I suppose it's a fine day for a ride, Captain Butler."

A pleased smile spread across his face. "It is, Miss Fryer, and should you not think it proper, which it's probably not, I could smuggle you out of town. They'd never even know I was here."

"Oh!" said Christine, a laugh escaping. She realized Hawthorne had probably reached Papa's study by now. "I don't think even you would be able to keep that secret."

He grinned and pulled her to him, and for a moment she thought he might kiss her but instead, he led her to his black thoroughbred prancing on the street corner.

"No carriage?"

"There's room for two."

Her cheeks burned at his intentions, but she did not care. It was too late. He helped her up and then joined her, his chest resting against her back as they trotted out of town past neighbors and then shopkeepers who stopped their sweeping to gape. She lifted her chin and kept her eyes straight ahead. It was her parade, and if they wanted to watch, then so be it.

"Well, I suppose those in the know will believe you've made an honest man out of me," Nathan whispered in her ear. She felt her lips curl into a smile as she gripped his hands over the reins.

They rode down the dirt road along the shore then turned inland. Nathan urged the horse into a cantor until he guided it off onto a game path that wound through thick vegetation. Christine soaked in the shade and salty breezes as his heart beat against her. Soon, the flat marsh spread open before them.

She spied the cottonwood grove and smiled. "I've missed this place," she admitted. Nathan drew the horse up with a gentle pull. He swung off and then reached for her. Christine kept her eyes on him as she fell into his arms. He set her gently on the ground then took her by the hand and peeled off her gloves. He buried them in his pockets.

"Come along." Nathan walked her through the marsh as the burnished sun glowed over the long grasses and tall wandering cranes. After they reached the inlet's point, their feet squelched in the wet earth until it inclined and became a footpath. He led her through more shade of ancient and yawning gnarled trees.

"I thought I would be hung," Nathan said in the peacefulness, "like my father, but by the government's hand."

Christine pulled off her hat. "Matty came. He told me the news. Papa would not let me go to the jail, but I... Well, I went down to his study and made a bargain. I had to give in to his demands."

"You agreed to marry Hawthorne."

"Yes, and Papa allowed me to come with Matty although he won't forgive me for going. His final threat was to send me away."

Nathan stopped. He took her by the shoulder, and his intense stare made her heart flip over. "When I saw you there my broken world came back together. I was sure it was crashing down in flames."

Christine steadied herself. "I would have done anything to save you. Anything at all." She bit her lip as his gaze wandered over her face.

"And that's why I came back to town," he replied in a hoarse tone.

"You mean because of Hawthorne?"

"I mean because I love you," he said. "I admire and respect you, Christine. Your stormy eyes and copper hair make me feel reckless. Do you know what that means?"

Her breath caught in her throat, tangled with hope.

"It means," he said with a small smile, "that I am as mad as my father and will not live without you. It would not be living at all."

She blinked in surprise as happiness did a minuet in her heart.

"See there?" In one smooth motion, Nathan waved his arm toward an opening in the trees. Christine spied a great gleaming white house beyond a split rail fence. Two giant oaks stood like sentinels on either wing of the home as clouds of gold and scarlet leaves danced around the lawn.

She put a hand to her heart. It was beautiful. "Clearwater?"

"There's a stream from a deep spring beyond the house that runs into the marsh. There may be no waterfalls, my Anya, but it's the cleanest clearest water to be found south of Savannah. It once fed the rice fields my grandfather grew here."

"It's a stunning house, Nathan. I'm sure your family would be very proud."

Nathan lowered his face so that his azure eyes were close enough for her to see tiny sea-blue flecks in them. "I only want *you* to be proud, Christine, and I want you to be my family."

Her eyes bloomed with tears, and she let them spill over. She bit her lip to keep from grinning all the way to her ears and reached for his arm.

"Marry me."

A wave of joy washed over her, tainted only by her father's regrets. "I'll have nothing to my name, Nathan, but I'd be honored," she said in a whisper, "because I love you... fervently." His eyes lit up with a strange glow, and the reply filled her with unspeakable joy that made her heart pound with anticipation.

With a nervous chuckle, Christine looked around in wonder. The distant house twinkled from the fading sun's last reflective rays. It looked like a fairyland. She took a deep breath and inhaled the familiar perfume of the marsh. "There's nothing I'd rather be than a Butler."

Nathan held her chin until she looked back into his eyes. He slowly moved his mouth to hers and pressed a warm kiss down on her lips. Her trembling knees gave way, and she sank into him as his arms went around her waist.

"Then I guess I may live awhile longer after all," he whispered in a teasing tone, "since I won't have to smuggle you out of Savannah."

Christine buried her face in his chest and inhaled the scent of the land and the sea that she so loved. "You may smuggle me to anywhere you wish, Captain Butler," she murmured.

He embraced her in silence as the marsh stretched its mysterious lavender arms around them, and the crickets and frogs began to sing their twilight song.

THE END

Don't miss *Gentlemen of the Coast Book Two*

Find your copy at Amazon.com.

About the Author

Danielle Thorne writes historical and contemporary romance from south of Atlanta, Georgia. Married for thirty years to the same fellow, she's the mother of four boys, two daughters-in-law, and she has two grandbabies. There are also cats involved.

Danielle is a graduate of Ricks College and BYU-Idaho. Besides writing pursuits, she's active in her church and community. Free time is filled with books, movies, too much yardwork, and not enough wandering the country or cruising the beautiful, blue seas. She's worked as an editor for Solstice and Desert Breeze Publishing and is the author of non-fiction for young adults.

Her first book with Harlequin's Love Inspired line will be out July 2020.

Visit Danielle at www.daniellethorne.com

You can also connect with Danielle at Facebook (Author Danielle Thorne), Twitter (@DanielleThorne), or Instagram (@authordaniellethorne).

More Books by Danielle Thorne

Historical

The Privateer of San Madrid

A Pirate at Pembroke

Proper Attire

Josette

Holiday

Brushstrokes and Blessings

Henry's Holiday Charade

Garland's Christmas Romance

Valentine Gold

Contemporary

Turtle Soup

By Heart and Compass

Death Cheater

Cheated

Non-fiction

Southern Girl, Yankee Roots

The Story of Andrew Jackson

The Story of Illinois Becoming a State

The Story of Queen Victoria 200 Years After Her Birth

Dear Reader, Before you go...

Please visit Amazon.com to share your thoughts
and review this book.
Thank you!

Made in the USA
Las Vegas, NV
04 May 2024